I0571167

KISS & MAKE UP

WILD CANYON ESTATES STORIES, #2

TE SHERIDAN

Kiss & Make Up

Wild Canyon Estates Stories

by

TE Sheridan

Contemporary Romance Novella

Published by TE Sheridan

Edited by A. Marie

Cover Photo: Deposit Photos

Cover Design by Redbird Designs

All Rights Reserved

Copyright © 2019 by TE Sheridan

ISBN#: 978-1-7334023-8-5

Names, characters, and incidents depicted in this book are products of the author's imagination or are used fictitiously. Any resemblance to actual events, or person, living or dead, is coincidental and not the intent of the author.

No part of this book may be reproduced in any form or by any electronic or mechanical means, including information storage and retrieval systems, without written permission from the author, except for the use of brief quotations in a book review.

1

Whitney Oliver heard the muted singular ring of her desk phone, but she didn't look. She couldn't. She couldn't tear her eyes away from her cell phone—the one she really shouldn't have out of her purse right now, while she was at work. Her brain had gone into overdrive when she saw the photo plastered all over Shawn Green's social media. He hadn't posted it, no, but *still*. The dark-haired chick with the nose ring and the spiked hair had tagged him in the picture, and besides, it was him *in* the photo, so he couldn't say he didn't know, it wasn't him, blah blah blah.

Okay, so the chick had clothes on. Sort of. If you counted that skimpy little black tank bra as a top. Whitney didn't. The picture was just from the waist up, so she couldn't see what else the chick had on. What she could see was that she had no tits, but she was either cold that night in Texas at the ball game—Whitney had never been to a Rangers game on a June evening, so she couldn't say if the girl should be cold—or she was pretty into Shawn Green.

The hell of it? If Whitney brought it up now? He would remind her that they broke up *before* he left for Texas on a boys' trip. He could also say that nothing happened, that he and his friends just hung out with some girls at the game, no big. He *had* said that. A few times now. He could also throw it back at her that she hadn't stayed at home pining away over him when he was gone. That she'd gone to a party with a friend and had some side action. Except that Whitney hadn't really told him that. She'd mentioned that Leslie Brewer had gone with her to a wedding shower, but she hadn't gone into details.

Why now, though? Why—three weeks after the fact—was this chick *just now* posting a picture of some random guy she met in Arlington, Texas and watched a baseball game and ate peanuts with? Was there more to the story? Were they still in contact? Shawn had dropped other names casually—the girls hanging on his buddies that night—but he hadn't mentioned anyone named Kori.

Whitney closed her eyes and drew a deep breath. It wasn't fair of her to get mad without asking him about the picture first. On the other hand, if she asked him about the picture, he would probably end up angry with her for bringing it up. Shouldn't she, though? Just to make sure? She might have been at that wedding shower; she might have played a few adult games, but she hadn't taken anyone home with her. She hadn't taken anyone to bed with her. Wasn't it acceptable for her to demand the same fidelity from him?

No. Not if they broke up before he left on the trip.

This time the muted ring of her desk phone jerked her out of her head and reminded her she was at work. She was in a professional business environment, and it certainly wasn't the place to stew over what Shawn might have done while he was gone. With a sad sigh, she leaned to her left to snatch the slim black receiver from the cradle and dropped her cell phone back in her purse as she did.

"Whitney Oliver." She tried but failed to pump some

energy into her voice. Six years. She and Shawn had been retracing the steps of this same old dance now for six years. He balked anytime the subject of marriage came up. Whitney hadn't wanted a baby when she was in high school or even fresh out of college, but she was eyeballing thirty as it approached down the horizon. She had planned to be married and *thinking about* children by twenty-seven.

She loved him. No denying that even though he made her mad as a hornet ten times a day, he could still make her weak in the knees with a smile. With his sleep-gruff voice when he awoke next to her in bed after the nights they spent together. With a bouquet of no-reason, no-special-day flowers. The warmth in his brown eyes when he looked at her from across a crowded room. The way they communicated without saying a word.

Feeling a little guilty for missing the call—wasting bank time on her phone—she placed the receiver back in the cradle, rubbed the skin under her eyes, and turned her attention back to her computer screen. While she'd had her back to the hall behind her cubicle, someone had left her paperwork to input data on seven new customer accounts. She cast a quick look at the time stamp in the top right corner of her monitor. Less than an hour to go. She would see Shawn later in the evening. No dinner plans; he would be on the golf course until after seven. Not even league night. Whitney enjoyed golf and played with him now and then. She didn't complain when he wiled away the hours at local courses. But there were certainly times she would like to see him when he wasn't available.

"Whitney."

She jumped and swiveled her chair around as Donna Jackson rounded the northern corner of her cubicle.

"Donna!" She hated the nervous laughter that seemed to bubble out of her whenever she bumped into Frank or

Donna Jackson now. Since the wedding shower she'd gone to with her best friend Leslie as her date, seeing Frank and Donna was a little awkward. Maybe she would agree that she had been a bit naïve to think those sorts of parties, those sorts of *things* didn't happen here in Rockfield. But she was an adult; and she did those sorts of things—with her boyfriend—and she watched that kind of stuff on adult channels and she knew it *happened*. Just…not here. Not at Wild Canyon Estates. With people she knew. Some that she knew well.

The wedding shower had worked in Leslie's favor, certainly. Whitney had been so excited for Leslie when she'd had her first date with Asher. It had been a whirlwind romance—of course, it was after starting off with the bang it did—but already, the two of them had hit a speed bump, weathered it, and stayed on course. They were happy. If Whitney knew Leslie—and she did—she'd believe her friend was falling in love with Asher Collins.

"What're you doing here?" Whitney hugged Donna and then rested her hands on the waist high cubicle wall. Donna used to work here at the bank as a customer service rep. That thought tickled Whitney all over again. She tamped down the little snort of laughter. Donna left the bank to accept an offer as a branch manager at another local bank. Frank, her husband, was a VP in real estate loans here. His office was on the other side of the building, but Whitney still bumped into him now and then.

"Lunch hour. Came by to see Frank for a second."

"Lunch? At three?" Whitney frowned. Her stomach was usually growling by ten in the morning.

"Staying busy, girl." Donna laughed off her concern. "First chance I had to get out for a minute."

"Better watch yourself. You'll be accused of espionage or something."

"I'm sleeping with the enemy," Donna reminded her. "Could be some big pillow talk going on."

Whitney blinked, stunned by the comment after the things she'd witnessed at Donna's house. She offered her friend an amused smile and nodded her agreement.

"Good point."

"I have something for you." Donna slipped her purse off her shoulder to hang from her wrist.

"For me?" Whitney shook her head. "Why me?"

Donna reached into the big leather bag and produced a crème-colored envelope with a flourish. Whitney, rooted where she stood, eyeballed the envelope with trepidation. Her name—and Shawn's—were written in elegant cursive over the front.

"What's this?" She swallowed hard, hesitant to take the envelope when Donna thrust it at her.

"It's an invitation." Donna shrugged and waved Whitney's question away. Whitney's heartbeat suddenly tripped and then raced, but she took the envelope. Her hand was steady, but inside she was shaking. Was she just automatically going to be invited to those parties now? True, the thing a few weeks ago was a wedding shower for a coworker. But still. According to Asher, Donna's nephew and Leslie's new boyfriend, Donna and Frank hosted adult entertainment parties often. She'd been intrigued the night of the shower, and once she'd had a few drinks, she had settled down and sort of had fun.

But. She wasn't sure she'd had enough fun to go back.

And she definitely wasn't sure she wanted Shawn at that kind of party. Not because she would prefer to keep it from him—the fact that she'd been at the shower and let a few guys feel her up when she played *Spin the Bottle*—but because she worried about how enthusiastically he would play along.

She didn't trust him.

Seriously. If she didn't trust him, they were through.

"Um." She licked her lips and nodded once. Donna watched her knowingly when their eyes met, but Whitney, embarrassed now by her own relationship and not the sexual nature of the parties, looked away quickly. "I'm not sure Shawn...and I..." She shrugged and tapped the corner of the envelope on the cubicle. "Thank you. For the invite."

"Maybe a night out at our place is exactly what you and Shawn need."

"You think dragging an alcoholic to a bar is a good idea?"

"Does he cheat?"

Whitney thought again of the picture she'd just seen on her phone. And reminded herself if anything had happened in Texas, it didn't count as cheating since she and Shawn broke up before he left.

"No." She smacked her lips together and shook her head, still reluctant to meet the older woman's eyes. "But."

"Maybe he needs to see the Whitney Oliver I did at Felicia's wedding shower." Donna raised her eyebrows suggestively.

"What? The one swapping spit with a bunch of strangers? Kissing her best friend?"

"No." Donna tugged her purse straps back up over her shoulder and folded her arms over her chest. The simple black silk blouse she wore was elegant and attractive. Certainly nothing about it to advertise the juicy, sexy parties she and her husband hosted. The wedding ring on her finger was hard to miss, too. Whitney fought the urge to rub her thumb over her bare ring finger. Seemed like after dating someone for so long, the bare ring finger was even more noticeable. "The one who didn't care what anyone thought of her. The beautiful girl smiling and laughing with friends and coworkers."

Wondering how to take Donna's comment, Whitney

drew in a deep breath. She wouldn't describe herself as an unhappy person, but she had definitely been down the night of the shower. She loved Leslie Brewer to the moon and back, but the couples shower was an event for couples, by definition. Was it wrong that she wanted to spend her weekends and evenings with her boyfriend? The same man who was happy to fuck her when he was in the mood but always needed to go on guys' trips and to football games and the golf course, and therefore didn't always have time for her?

As stunning as the shower had been—wasn't often you walked up to a portable bar and watched people skinny dip while you waited for your drink—she did have fun. She had laughed. Shared some terrible kisses. Some good kisses. Drew some dirty pictures and assembled some dirty words with game tiles. More than one guy had had his hand in her shirt—though only one actually touched her breast, the other ran out of time before he found the nerve—but it hadn't been a turn on for her. Fun and flirty and sexy, sure. But she loved Shawn, and at the end of the night, when she and Leslie left the party, she had no desire to hook up with anyone there.

What would Shawn do? At a party like that? Would he take advantage of the smorgasbord? The pass to cheat? Or would it just be a night out, and then the two of them would go home together and have sex—they had good sex; she couldn't complain about the way he treated her in bed. But would a party like that spark something new between them? Is that why the married couples played along?

"Just promise me you'll think about it."

Whitney stirred to life at Donna's words, flustered again by the state of her personal relationship and Donna's intuition. She cleared her throat and nodded, managed to muster up a small smile, and backed away from the gray fabric wall.

"I will," she promised and almost meant it.

Relieved when Donna said goodbye and walked away

without further small talk, Whitney sank to her chair and held her breath for a second. She heard Donna talking to Elin French at the next cubicle. She listened for a second, but when the only words she picked up were soccer and hat trick, she tuned them out.

Maybe Donna was right. Maybe a party the likes of her and Frank's was just what she and Shawn needed. For now, she tucked the invitation, unopened, into her purse, ignored the siren's call of her phone—she was dying to know if Shawn had commented on the picture—and turned her face, if not her attention, to her computer screen.

Later this evening, she would open the invitation and see if they were even free the night of the party. And then, maybe, she would casually toss the idea out to Shawn and see if he was interested. Of course, if he said yes, she was going to have to give him a little more detail about the couples shower she'd gone to with Leslie.

But she'd cross that bridge if and when she got to it.

2

Whitney dropped her oversized purse on the counter and tossed her keys beside it when she got home. Her afternoon—that last ninety minutes—had crawled by, her heart and mind heavy with the realization that she and Shawn had no future. Not unless she was ready to give up her dreams of a family.

She stood for a moment, head ducked with her chin to her chest, trying to talk herself through the tears. It was a waste of time to cry over what she and Shawn had and didn't have. She'd settled for far too little for far too long, and she was the fool for it. Not Shawn. Emotions finally under control, she drew a deep breath and then fished her phone and the invitation from her purse.

The invitation, she simply put on the counter, unopened. She'd flip-flopped on that whole thing for the remainder of her day, too. Go to the party? For an experiment? But wasn't that the same as testing Shawn? And if she was testing Shawn because she didn't trust him, wasn't that the end of the line for them? But what if it did light a spark between them? What if it changed something for the better?

She smoothed her fingertips over the envelope, eyes on their names written there together, and reminded herself again that she and Shawn didn't need any added spark in the bedroom. They'd never had an issue with sex. Just the part in a relationship where they committed—he committed—to marriage and forever. Going to Donna and Frank's party might light up the next few nights and create some sort of sexual frenzy for them, but it wasn't going to magically change Shawn's views on marriage.

She hadn't bothered to open it yet. No idea what the date of the party was. Now, she took her phone from her purse and stood for another few moments of indecision. Look again? At the picture? See if he commented? Or not? Why torture herself?

She put her phone down and walked away. Eye balled it from across the kitchen as she filled a glass with water and took a healthy drink. Her stomach a twisted mess of nerves, she stalked across the open living room to her bedroom to change clothes, feeling ridiculously righteous because she'd had the willpower to leave her phone in the kitchen.

Whitney stripped out of her emerald green trousers and the gold silk blouse, but rather than kick the garments into a pile on the floor by her bed so she could hurry back out to her phone, she forced herself to pick up both pieces and lay them in her dry-cleaning pile. She studiously ignored her reflection in the mirror of her dresser as she dug a pair of athletic shorts from her drawer and stepped into them. Her eyes glimpsed her smooth belly and average breasts in the crème silk bra, but feeling stubborn, she turned her back to the mirror and eyed her room instead.

She would never be a lingerie model, but she'd never been the type of girl to disparage over her body or her looks, either. Shawn told her often enough that she was beautiful, that she was sexy, and she believed he thought so. She even believed her loved her. She just didn't believe he loved her the same way she loved him.

He spent the night last night, and they'd lingered a bit after the alarm went off this morning, so she hadn't had time to make her bed. She stared at the comforter and baby blue sheet, tangled together at the foot of the bed. The night they'd made the sex video—she still couldn't believe she'd told Leslie that—the sheets had been black silk. She'd lit candles around the room, and Shawn had tossed a few rose petals on the bed. Instead of being sexy, they'd found it funny, and they'd laughed about it while they tried to make out.

Eventually, it got hot and heavy, as usual. Watching the recording later had been surreal. Wasn't anything like she'd seen in the movies, and yet, it had been sexy as hell, and it still turned her on to watch it. They'd recorded it on her phone, and now it was on a file on her laptop. Now and then they watched it together.

If they broke up again, she should delete it. Trust issues and stuff. Then again, Shawn probably wouldn't care if she ever decided to be vindictive and post the video on social media. He had an impressive body, and he knew how to use it, and women would love to watch the muscles in his shoulders and his ass move under his smooth skin as he pumped his hips over hers to rub his cock in all the right places.

Just thinking about it again aroused her. She decided she might keep it after all, and then she grabbed an old t-shirt and yanked it on and quickly made her bed. Maybe she just wouldn't welcome him back tonight.

When she realized she was thinking of cutting him off just to punish him for the picture some chick named Kori posted, she flipped the bedroom light off and returned to the kitchen. Her phone hadn't moved. She eyed it suspiciously, as if it might throw itself at her, when she went to the refrigerator to find something for dinner. But it was almost as if it was burning a hole in her back, begging her to pick it up and take a peek, and finally, after grabbing a bell pepper and the container of mushrooms, she backed away from the fridge. Not caring anymore that she was being jealous and immature, she dropped the vegetables on the counter by the sink and rushed back to her phone.

The picture was still there. And yes, Shawn had commented. He'd liked it—bad enough—and he'd said awesome night. With two exclamation points. Shawn Green didn't do exclamation points. Ever. Sickened by the possibilities of what had made the night so *awesome!!* she returned to her dinner, her appetite gone.

Still stewing over the picture and Shawn's comment and what might have happened to make that night awesome, Whitney didn't even look when she heard the door open. She pulled a cutting board from the cabinet and set it on the table, freezing when Shawn moved up behind her and ringed his arm around her neck.

"Hey." He kissed the top of her head and leaned closer to squeeze her. "How was your day?"

Not ready to launch into the dark, circular thoughts she'd chased all day, she only shrugged and nodded. "Good. Yours?"

He spun her around to face him and settled his hands on her hips. Whitney felt the sharp edge of her frustration soften a bit as he dipped his head to kiss her.

"Better now."

She laughed softly and turned back to the cutting board. She wasn't ready to delve into the same old argument again, but she didn't particularly have the energy to pretend everything was great, either.

"What's this?"

She glanced at him over her shoulder to find him tapping the elegant crème envelope.

"Um." She shook her head and pulled her eyes from his. "Just a party invitation."

"Yeah?" He picked it up and flipped it over. "From who? You haven't even opened it."

"Someone at the bank," she mumbled. Stomach tied in knots, she pulled a knife from the drawer jammed with kitchen utensils and started slicing the bell pepper.

"Yeah?" Shawn sounded interested. She glanced at him as he leaned over to prop his elbows on the countertop. "Who? Anyone I know?"

"Frank and Donna Jackson."

He shook his head as he turned the envelope over and over in his hands. It was almost funny, the way he studied the fancy envelope, as if it might contain a Valentine from a long, unrequited crush.

"Name sounds familiar," he said quietly, but the deep groove between his eyes told her he didn't remember them well. "Can I open it?"

"Sure." She shrugged. Now or never, she thought. She could be stuck here forever in this stagnant relationship, somewhat content, but never really happy. Or she could push the envelope—she snorted softly—and see if anything changed. Because she had no idea what to expect, she crossed the room to stand by him. The familiar, crisp scent of his cologne drew her closer.

He shot her a quick look as he ripped the seal and then tugged the crème-colored 4x6 card from the envelope. When their eyes met, he grinned, and it hit her again that going to a party like this might mean watching her lover with someone else. She wasn't sure she could do it.

"What's wrong?" he asked her when she turned her eyes away.

"Nothing." She stood near enough to him to feel the heat from his body, but she didn't touch him. Fingers spread over the counter, she looked at the card with him. Simple and elegant, like Donna herself. Black cursive type inviting them to a party at Wild Canyon Estates. Adults only.

"Do they have kids?" Shawn asked her.

"Yeah."

"Hmm." He turned the card over, but the back was blank. "Wild Canyon. That's that really fancy neighborhood, isn't it? Like…on the west side of town?"

"It is." She nodded.

"Next Friday," he announced. "Do you want to go?"

Whitney whooshed out a deep breath and rolled her lips inward.

"I don't know."

"Wait. Isn't that the address where you went to that party with Leslie? The shower thing?"

"It is." She sighed. "Their parties are adults only."

"Okay." He put the card and envelope down and wiggled his eyebrows at her. Whitney felt a streak of heat in her face, and she wondered if he understood what she was saying. Had Leslie told him? Asher? They'd been out with them twice since Asher had decided to move to Rockfield, but she hadn't considered that Asher might mention the nature of the shower, the parties to Shawn. "We can leave the kids at home for a night."

Her shoulders sagged with relief when she realized he was just teasing her, but at the same time, his words made that ache inside yawn and stretch a bit bigger. She would love to be in a situation where they needed a sitter to go out for a night. The fact that he didn't just know that hurt her even more.

"It's a lot of sex, Shawn."

"Sex." He moved now. Stepped around the end of the

cabinets to lean on them and watch her with a horrified look on his face. "You had sex at the wedding shower? That you went to with Leslie?"

The question hit her smack in the face, because while she hadn't had sex with Leslie, she had most definitely shared a very intimate, very open-mouthed kiss with her best friend.

"I didn't," she answered truthfully, "but I could have. If I had wanted to."

"What do you mean?"

"The shower games."

"Wow." He rested his hands on the counter at his sides and shrugged dramatically. "Sounds like showers have changed some since my mom used to go to them all the time."

"From what I gather, they host parties like this a lot. They have a group of friends who host parties like this. It just so happened that Donna put on a shower for Felicia, and it was that kind of shower."

"So. What're you telling me?" He folded his arms over his chest. "It's just a big orgy?"

"No. At least the shower wasn't." She leaned into the counter at her back, propped her hands at her sides, and hoisted herself up to sit. "Everybody got a passport. You could get it stamped for playing games."

"Damn." Shawn sounded intrigued, maybe a bit bummed that he'd missed out on the fun and games, but not angry. "What was the prize?"

"A gift card." She shook her head dismissively. "I wasn't interested in winning."

"But you played the games?"

"Some of them."

He nodded.

"Okay."

"Okay?" she snapped. "Really?"

"We broke up before I went to Texas," he reminded her. "So. Whatever you did at the party is your business."

Which translated to whatever he'd done with Kori—the chick in the picture—was his business.

"Do you wanna go?" She jammed the guilt back down her throat and licked her lips. "See what it's all about?"

"Will it be...the same kind of party?"

"I don't know." She shrugged. "Asher told Leslie that they have adult parties. That's all I know."

"And what would we do? Watch other people get naked?"

"At the shower, it was anything goes. Married couples. Strangers. Young kids fresh out of college. People who could probably retire. Games as easy as *Dirty Word Scrabble* all the way to skinny dipping in the rain."

"Wow." Shawn nodded again. "Do you wanna go?"

His enthusiasm, even though he tried to contain it, filled her with dread. But she reminded herself that if he wanted other women, this was a good way to find out. And walk away before she threw any more of her life away on their relationship.

"Kind of."

"Will it be the same people?"

"I don't know." She shook her head. "Why?"

"Just wondering if there's someone you're hoping to bump into again."

Whitney snorted. "Shawn, the hottest kiss I had that night was Leslie."

"You had all that opportunity and all you got was a sweet little kiss on the cheek?"

"I didn't say that," she argued quietly. "I said the hottest kiss was Leslie, and no, it wasn't a kiss on the cheek."

3

Because Whitney knew herself well enough to know she would change her mind about the party, she texted Leslie the following morning, as soon as Shawn left. He had stayed over, despite the fact that she'd made the bed hoping he would feel less inclined to stay, that pulling the comforter back to crawl in would be too much work for him. Not in the mood for sex, Whitney had called upon her inner actress to fake an orgasm to get it over with and then laid awake stewing over what Shawn might have done that *awesome night!!* in Texas. Shawn, on the other hand, had pulled her close to spoon and gone to sleep instantly.

Whitney's phone chimed with Leslie's response the second she set it down to pour the coffee Shawn had made for her before he left. Tired after a night of tossing and turning, she rubbed sleep from her eyes with her left hand — she'd finally drifted off after two—and stretched to replace the glass carafe on the burner with the other. She picked her mug up to sip from it, closed her eyes for a second, and relived Shawn's goodbye—a quick kiss on her forehead, his offer of coffee, and his promise to call her later—before looking at the screen.

You're going to the party.

Whitney stared at her phone silently for a moment and then huffed out a deep breath and picked it up again. She wanted to go, not because she was interested in messing around, but because something about Donna's suggestion that it might help things between her and Shawn intrigued her. On the other hand, the thought of taking Shawn to a party like that terrified her.

Which is why she texted Leslie. As much as Leslie liked Shawn, she was Whitney's best friend, and as such, would give her the gentle nudge she needed to commit to the plan and follow through. Even if that plan did involve a major life change.

I'm not sure I want to.

She carried her phone and coffee to the bathroom, put both on the sink, and leaned into the shower stall to turn the water on. Some mornings, he stuck around longer. If they were up early enough, they had breakfast together. Sometimes she served fresh fruit and toasted bagels; other times, Shawn fixed omelets and toast. He wasn't much of a newspaper guy, but he liked to watch the news in the morning when he was here.

Unless they were still in bed.

He kept a toothbrush here; she kept one at his place. In fact, they both had their own drawers and closet space in each other's homes. Whitney had been careful not to rush that part of their relationship. In the beginning, she had worried that he might balk if she started leaving things at his place, so she waited until he suggested it. They'd been together just over a year when he brought it up. It was a winter morning, and though she dreaded it, Whitney had to climb from his warm bed and dress to go home and get ready for work. Laughing, they'd wrestled naked in his bed, as he held her down, teasing her with pleas to stay and she fought him because she had to be at work on time.

She stripped her pajamas off now and dropped them and the blue silk panties to the floor. A smile lingered on her lips as she took another sip of her coffee and then stepped into the shower. Shawn had begged her with a goofy cartoonish voice to stay, and then he'd pinned her arms over her head and licked her skin from the hollow of her throat to a spot just below her belly button. When she bucked under him and moaned her displeasure at his stopping point, he'd turned his head and nipped at her hip. Patted her bare ass and climbed from bed and looked at her with a cheeky smile. His cock, hard and ready for her, had belied his breezy tone when he suggested they'd have more time to play in the mornings if she left some of her things at his place.

That had been five years ago. She'd offered him the same at her place, and they took advantage of the space and the extra time, but nothing more had really changed. Her phone chimed as she lathered her hair with shampoo. It would be Leslie, but still, Whitney was curious about what she would say, so she moved through her shower routine quickly.

Ten minutes later, she stood at the sink again with her towel tucked around her body and her wet hair hanging down the middle of her back.

Are you worried about telling him about the shower? Playing Spin the Bottle?

She wasn't. Not really. She'd kissed a few people, and someone had felt her up—sort of—but somehow, she knew her night was nothing compared to whatever *awesome!!* things he'd done that night.

No. Just don't want to watch Shawn do something with someone else.

She waited for Leslie to call her on it. To nail down the

fact that if she was worrying about Shawn messing around, it was time to call it quits. Thinking about walking away from a six-year relationship was different from actually doing it. From ending things. Cutting the ties for good. But this dating thing wasn't what she'd hoped to be doing by this age, either.

Suddenly her small bathroom erupted with a radar sound. The blaring ringtone startled her; she nearly knocked her coffee mug over as she reached for her phone. She half hoped it would be Shawn calling, but there was no reason for him to call now, so Leslie's name on her screen shouldn't be a disappointment.

"Stop thinking."

"I just got out of the shower."

"Okay but stop thinking. Just go."

"But what if—"

"Whitney." Leslie spoke in a firm voice. Whitney sagged and rested her towel-wrapped ass on the sink at her back. She couldn't bear to look at herself in the mirror as she listened to her friend talk. Leslie often gave her pep talks about Shawn, about her love life. He and Leslie were friends; Shawn was a likeable guy. But Whitney also knew that if Leslie were dating him, she would have ended the relationship a long time ago. Shawn had strung Whitney along long enough that she expected it, and though Leslie was never harsh, she often pointed out to Whitney that she was only going to get what she settled for. "Call it an experiment."

"Some experiments fail," Whitney mumbled.

"I know." Leslie softened her tone. "Maybe seeing other men appreciate you will knock some sense into him."

Whitney laughed, though her stomach twisted at the thought. She had no idea what sort of format this party would be, but she doubted it would be shower games. For all she knew, it would be an orgy, and everyone there would be walking around naked. Whitney didn't care for the thought of other people looking at her any more than she did other people looking at Shawn.

"I'm not suggesting you mess around. But you're beautiful, Whit. Inside and out. Maybe if Shawn sees you in a different light, he'll realize what's at risk."

"Isn't it kind of sad that he has to see me in a different light to realize that?"

Even as the whispered words slipped from her mouth, Whitney cringed. Of course, it was sad. Of course, it said a lot about the state of their relationship if Shawn had to be jealous to remember why he loved her.

"Maybe." Leslie's answer surprised Whitney. "Then again, maybe it doesn't hurt to be reminded now and then what's important."

"I'm not gonna go fuck some other guy just to make him jealous," Whitney argued. She didn't want to play games, and she damned sure wasn't interested in hooking up with a stranger.

"Nothing says you have to fuck anybody," Leslie said quietly. "But what's the harm in going to the party? Have a drink or two. Talk to Donna. Flirt a little. Give away a kiss or two."

Whitney sighed.

"I'll come over so we can pregame before you go."

"Now I'm really scared," Whitney whispered, but Leslie's laughter was contagious, and she was giggling before she ended the call.

———

SHAWN DROVE to Wild Canyon Estates, and though it wasn't a long drive, Whitney was relieved she wouldn't have to concentrate. Nerves about the night ahead buzzed in her belly like the powerlines over the open lot where she and the neighborhood kids had played when they were little. She smoothed the hem of her short dress over her legs. Leslie had come to her house earlier, before Shawn arrived, to provide moral support while Whitney dressed for the party. Whitney was the fashion guru, but the dress had been Leslie's suggestion. The deep green tank dress was soft and clingy, and according to Leslie, the color made her eyes pop. Leslie had also coached her to forgo a bra. The sway of her breasts and her nipples pressed into the soft fabric caught Shawn's eyes instantly. He'd been so interested he missed the wink and grin Leslie had aimed at her.

They arrived at Wild Canyon as two other cars parked in front of Frank and Donna's house. Those couples seemed to know each other; the women were chatty as they walked up the cobblestone drive. Though both couples were older, Whitney found herself eyeing the women—both ash blondes —critically and wondering if Shawn found them attractive.

It had been raining when she and Leslie had come for the wedding shower; and they'd been laughing as they climbed from Whitney's car and hauled ass up to the front door in a crazy attempt to stay dry. Now, she took the time to look around and admire the immaculate yard and landscaping. Evening sun through the boughs of the trees dappled the vivid green yard with spots of lighter green and yellow. The house itself was an imposing brick structure set atop a small crest, the house at the end of the cul-de-sac, and it owned the street like the belle of the ball. Whitney wondered if their neighbors were aware of what sorts of things went on at the parties, or if some of their guests were neighbors. No time to worry too much over it, however, as she blinked and found herself staring at the wide, wooden door, framed by frosted glass sidelights. The interior of the house was all majestic marble and honey blonde cabinetry, but Whitney was in no hurry to get inside now that they were here.

"Last chance to change your mind." She glanced at Shawn.

"Let's do this, Whit." He nodded toward the doorbell, so Whitney raised her hand and pushed the round button with her index finger. She wondered if she would be single again, permanently, come Monday morning.

Donna answered the door tonight, and her face lit up with a brilliant smile of welcome when she saw Whitney and Shawn there on the porch.

"Whitney." She reached for her, grabbed her hand, and gave her a gentle tug. Whitney stepped inside not only the house but also Donna's embrace. "Shawn, hi. Not sure if you remember me, but I'm Donna."

"It's good to see you again." Shawn flashed that charming smile, the one that did things to Whitney's body that no one else's touch had done. He shook Donna's hand, and then, once in the living room with other party guests, they bumped into Frank, and he repeated the gesture and the words with him.

"Donna was really hoping you guys would make it," Frank told her. Bald, and big and wide like a pro football player, Frank slung his arm around her waist and gave her a squeeze. Whitney noticed Shawn's eyes dip first to her breasts as they swung in her dress and then to Frank's hand where it rested on her hip. "Bronson's at the bar. We'll get started in just a few minutes."

"Thanks, Frank." Whitney nodded. Frank gave her another quick squeeze, and then he was gone, leaving a shell-shocked Shawn gaping at her. She plastered on a bright smile and looked around, finding the sand marbled-tiled room just as she remembered it. When she brought her gaze back around to Shawn, he opened his mouth to speak, stuttered, and tried again. She almost laughed; it wasn't funny, not really, but he hadn't even seen anything shocking, and already, he was uncomfortable.

"Bronson?" He shook his head.

"Bartender out back," she explained. She reached for his hand and felt a rush of warmth—and she hated to admit it, but relief—when Shawn linked his fingers with hers.

"They have a bar?"

"Well, it's a little portable bar," she told him.

"And a bartender?"

"Yep." She nodded and looked around as they made their way across the cavernous room. Several faces looked familiar, and of course, she had kissed a few of the mouths she saw now. No one appeared embarrassed, so she tried hard not to. Shawn, on the other hand, looked around the room as if he was a toddler, being led into a big circus with scary clowns, which Whitney found funny, being that everyone was still fully clothed and behaving properly. They could have been at any party at the moment. She couldn't resist teasing him as they stepped through the French doors that led outside to the patio, where still more people mingled. "He's kind of sexy," she told him.

"Who?" Shawn asked quickly as he swung his head back around to look at her.

"The bartender." She rolled her eyes.

"Did you kiss him?"

"No." She shook her head, but she felt a jolt of heat slide through her when Bronson the bartender looked at her and grinned in recognition.

"Where's the other sidekick?" he asked. "She's prettier. No offense, man." He shifted his gaze to Shawn and offered him an apologetic laugh.

Shawn held his hands up in surrender. "None taken. Leslie's much easier on the eyes than I am."

"Screaming Blue Viking?" Bronson asked Whitney.

"What the hell is a Screaming Blue Viking?" Shawn asked as Whitney hid a grin and shook her head.

"Chocolate raspberry martini?" Bronson tried again.

"Please."

"But do you need a shot?" he asked as he set about mixing her drink. Whitney rested her elbows on the bar, a little bit delighted at the feel of the soft material of her dress rubbing over her bare nipples. Even so, the night ahead loomed daunting and uncertain, and she nodded to tell Bronson she definitely needed a shot.

"Where is your pretty friend tonight?" he asked as he poured chocolate liqueur into a cocktail shaker.

"Leslie?" She arched her eyebrows. Was she supposed to talk about previous party guests with the bartender? What if that guest was dating the hosts' nephew? Was that okay to talk about?

"Hot date?"

"Yes." She nodded instantly, grateful for his rescue. Either he knew Asher and knew he and Leslie were together, or he realized he'd committed a Frank and Donna party foul and was doing the right thing by giving her an easy out.

"That the pool?"

Whitney turned when Shawn elbowed her in the ribs. Even though he spoke in a whisper, Whitney shot Bronson a quick peek as her cheeks flushed. She didn't want to give him the impression that she was some doe-eyed innocent girl who had gone home after the shower and gushed at all the nudity and sex she'd seen. Either Bronson didn't hear Shawn, or he was pretending he hadn't heard him as he set a bottle of vodka on the bar and then put the lid on the shaker.

Shawn's eyeballs burned a hole in the side of her face, though, and she didn't want Bronson to catch her watching him, so she quickly turned back to Shawn and nodded. He blinked, still having difficulty processing everything she had told him and what he was now seeing.

"Thank you," Whitney told Bronson as he passed first her martini to her and then slid the shot glass over the bar.

"Tequila," he told her. "Actually meant to be chilled and sipped from a champagne flute, but desperate times call for desperate measures."

She snorted an unladylike laugh and then covered her mouth with her fingers. From the corner of her eye, she saw Shawn roll his eyes.

"Were you and Leslie pre-gaming?" he asked, but he was grinning with her now. The question, so reminiscent of what Leslie had said about coming over to help her get ready, brought a sense of longing to her. She didn't want to trade Shawn for Leslie, but she did wish her friend was here, too.

"What can I get you?"

"Beer." Shawn tapped a brown longneck bottle on display.

"Bronson." The bartender told him as he dug into a cooler and retrieved an icy cold bottle. He twisted the top off and handed it to Shawn.

"I'm Shawn." He took the beer and shook Bronson's hand. "Interesting set up."

"You have no idea," Bronson said with a small knowing laugh. "It's always a good time. But you gotta play by the rules."

"And do you play?" Shawn took a pull of the beer. Whitney watched his eyes do an intense slide over Bronson's close-cropped hair and sun-kissed skin and then shift over to her. Was he jealous? Seriously? Because she'd said Bronson was sexy? Or was he starting to worry about the things she might have done at the wedding shower?

"Used to." Bronson nodded, but he didn't offer further explanation. "Now I get paid to hand out drinks and watch it all."

Whitney glanced over her other shoulder at the edge of the garage. Leslie and Asher had met briefly on the other side of the garage for a goodnight kiss that turned into a whole lot more. She wondered if Bronson ever left his station at the bar. If he might have seen what Leslie and Asher had done. If it would have bothered Leslie if he had.

"Damn." Shawn laughed and groaned in commiseration with Bronson. "Bet you go home with blue balls some nights."

"Shawn!" Whitney whirled around to glare at her boyfriend. Wide-eyed innocence stared back at her.

"What?" He shrugged. "Guys watch stuff like that, they get hard, Whit. You know that. Imagine watching it like this." He tossed his hands out as if to encompass the backyard and the house and the live sex acts that he hadn't even seen yet.

Whitney tossed her shot back and slammed the glass down on the bar.

"He's not wrong," Bronson told her when she shot him a quick look.

"Men." She shook her head and rolled her eyes. "I'm going back inside."

"Nice to meet you," Shawn told Bronson as he turned to follow her inside. "What kind of bug is up your ass?" he followed close enough behind her that he could speak and no one else would hear him.

"It's not really good etiquette to walk around talking to other guys about blue balls and hard-ons at a party like this. This isn't a frat party, Shawn. These are people I work with. Family people. The keyword here is discretion."

"I'm sorry," he mumbled. She stopped just inside the spacious, open floor plan where the kitchen was open to the living room which appeared to roll into what could be a dining area and yet another small alcove where tonight there was an accent chair, though Whitney couldn't be sure there had been anything there the last time she had been here. Frank and Donna stood in the center of the room, talking quietly to each other. Walking so closely behind her, Shawn bumped into Whitney. Rather than move away, though, he slid a possessive arm around her waist and grinded his cock into the small of her back. He was hard already.

"I think we're about ready to begin," Donna announced. When the party conversation didn't dim at all, Frank stuck his thumb and finger in his mouth and pierced the room and Whitney's head with a shrill whistle.

"That was pure frat party." Shawn nuzzled her neck. She shivered at the press of his cold lips on her skin and rested her head on his chest as the crowd fell quiet.

"Okay." Donna looked at the semi-circle of people around her and Frank and offered them all a big smile. "If you've been here before and you've been invited back, it means you observed the unwritten rules of discretion here at House Jackson."

"Hear, hear!" someone called from the back of the room.

Donna laughed and lifted her mixed drink in a salute.

"We appreciate that, and please know that we also enjoyed having you here. We're all friends here, and we all continue to respect each other's privacy once we leave the house. Here's how we're going to do tonight."

There was a rush of catcalls and shouts for Donna to take it off. She and Frank both laughed; Whitney marveled at the fact that neither of them appeared embarrassed by the teasing. Or by the party agenda in general.

"I have a passport for each of you." She waved a stack of cards in her other hand. "Your first name only is on the front of each card. On the back, you will find your passport has already been stamped with a puzzle piece. Your job is to find a person whose stamp is an interlocking puzzle piece."

Whitney felt a pang of regret. She didn't want to do this.

No way in hell could she watch Shawn preen for other women. If she saw him slip into another room with someone else, the unknown would eat away at her and make her crazy. If he stayed in the main area and some chick went down on him or flipped her skirt up and straddled him to take a ride, she might grab a handful of that girl's hair and yank it out.

"Once you find a puzzle piece that would fit yours, have a drink together. Talk a bit. If you want."

Someone roared with laughter. Shawn squeezed her hip. She knew he was telling her that the laughter was also frat party level.

"If you don't know your match and you're talking, please get to know each other."

"D, baby, you're killing me!"

Whitney turned to look for the owner of the deep voice in the back of the room.

"No long-winded sessions on philosophy, Jarvis," Donna said with a laugh. "Talk about your limits. Hard limits. Things you're willing to try. Some of you have no limits, and some of you are simply here to play around a bit. Anything goes. It's all completely up to you, but please, be sure you know when you pair up, what you and your partner want."

"This is fucking real." Shawn ghosted his lips over Whitney's neck again, leaving her long, loose curls down to hide his face. She simply nodded.

"As always, the rooms on the main floor other than the master bedroom are available. Doors can be locked if you prefer to lock them. The backyard is also fair territory. And the main area, if you don't mind an audience."

"Is this what the shower was?" Shawn asked quietly.

"No." Whitney turned her head slightly toward him. "I told you about it."

"Damn, Whitney." He took a deep breath.

Donna and Frank were now making the rounds to hand

out the passports. Whitney held her breath, wishing she and Shawn's stamps would be interlocking puzzle pieces. Maybe the two of them sneaking off to the bathroom in a strange house would be a fun little thrill that upped the sexual tension and intensified the orgasms, and then they could just go home.

To *her* place.

Not home. She and Shawn didn't have one home. Suddenly remembering why she'd wanted to come, she stood up straight and sipped her drink. Bronson had coated the rim of her glass with chocolate. She licked it now as she turned to look Shawn in the eyes.

"Are you sure?" he asked her.

"Yeah." She nodded.

"What're your limits?" He curled his fingers around her wrist, but at the same time, Whitney felt another hand on her shoulder, and she looked up at Donna's big smile.

"Ready loves?" Donna asked with an exaggerated wag of her eyebrows. "Trust me. It's fun. It's just all in fun. And it makes even the really good stuff that much better."

What were her limits? Whitney wondered as Donna handed her a passport. On the front, her name was written in Donna's elegant cursive. She flipped it over to see the backside, wondering what Shawn's limits were. Her stamped puzzle piece was a corner piece with tabs on each side.

She didn't want to have sex with someone else. Even if Donna and Frank and Bronson and anyone else in the world said it was all in fun, Whitney wasn't interested. But she wasn't sure she wanted to be so transparent with Shawn. Why not make him curious? And would it just be curiosity, or was he worried?

Shawn mumbled to Donna to thank her when she handed him a passport. Whitney tried to swallow a rush of uncertainty when he flipped his card over. Though his puzzle piece had a straight edge, it also had two tabs which made it impossible to interlock with hers. Of course, their pieces weren't going to match. Whether that was by Donna's design or just fate, she'd known that would happen, hadn't she?

"Whit?" He tipped his head at her in askance. She flashed her card at him and shook her head, almost giddy with relief when she saw panic in his eyes.

"Catch up with you later, okay?" She leaned toward him and brushed her lips over the corner of his mouth. He touched her; his fingers brushed the back of her arm as she stepped away from him in search of someone else. Leslie had told her to walk away from Shawn tonight without a second glance and just enjoy herself. While the thought terrified her, she figured she'd come this far. Might as well take her best friend's advice.

"Hey. Whitney. Right?"

She froze in her tracks, near the French door. She had planned to slip outside for a bit of fresh air before jumping into the mix. When she looked over her shoulder to identify who spoke to her, she caught a glimpse of Shawn talking to a redhead at Frank and Donna's kitchen island. They were just talking, but Whitney had to wonder if they were discussing limits and maybe favorite positions. Rather than give into the ache in the pit of her belly and go rushing out the front door to run home and sulk, Whitney turned her full attention to the guy who had stopped her.

She had kissed him the night of her friend's wedding shower. Shorter than Shawn—scratch that—*her height*, his silver-rimmed square glasses and salt and pepper hair gave him a quiet, mature look. His hand had been one of three in her shirt, but he hadn't been the guy to touch her breast.

"Evan." His grin was warm and friendly; Whitney wondered if her drink—or maybe the shot of tequila—put the twinkle in his eye. Or if maybe he found her amusing.

Great. Just what she needed: Shawn having the time of his life with some hot redhead while she amused this guy with her backwoods naivete.

"May I?" He nodded at the passport in her hand. The thought of what was supposed to follow, what all of these people were going to do in just minutes, flustered her. She nearly dropped the card, but Evan reached to catch it at the same time she did. The brush of his fingers over hers drew a nervous laugh, and her belly twisted with nerves and something that felt like anticipation when she saw that their stamped puzzle pieces could be interlocking.

"You were heading outside," he reminded her. "Need a drink refill?"

"No." She shook her head. "I was just going to get some air."

"Mind if I join you?"

"No."

She didn't mind. She didn't give in to the urge to turn around and look for Shawn, either. She liked this guy okay. She'd liked him okay at the shower. He was attractive. Hadn't tasted like garlic—Leslie got that one—and he hadn't crammed his tongue down her throat with all greed and little finesse, either. As they walked, Evan rested his hand against the small of her back. Maybe it was a possessive move, but this guy made it feel more like he was protecting her.

Whitney cast a quick look around the backyard. One couple was already stripping down by the pool. Bronson was whipping up some kind of frozen drink. Evan watched a petite dark-haired woman who appeared to be hanging on every word of a tall, good-looking black guy. Whitney wasn't sure she needed protecting, except maybe from herself. She had been the one to bring that invitation home. Maybe she was uncomfortable now, but she had no one to blame for being here but herself. If she'd wanted to, she could've tossed the invitation before Shawn ever came over the other night.

"Are you married?" he asked as they wandered aimlessly over the winding sidewalk that led them around two lush, beautiful gardens set back from the house. Whitney wasn't privy to bank salaries, but apparently Frank or Donna or both of them made a bit more money than she did. She couldn't imagine a day when she could afford a home like this.

Then again, she would be happy with the home she was in now. If Shawn lived there with her.

"No." She shook her head. "But we've been together six years."

"Mmm."

Evan's simple murmur drew her attention. When he realized she was looking at him, he lifted an eyebrow.

"Maybe this will push him to make a move."

"Would it?" she asked him, suddenly anxious to hear a guy's point of view on the subject.

"I'm probably not the person to ask." He twitched his lips apologetically. "My wife loves these parties. Me? I like barbeques. A good volleyball game in the backyard. A cold beer."

"So, you do this for her?"

"I guess I do." He nodded. "Don't get me wrong. It's fun. The people are interesting." He laughed softly. "Beyond the obvious. But. Sometimes I wonder if she would stay with me if I put a stop to these nights."

Whitney bit her lip. "How long have you been married?"

"Twenty-seven years," he answered. "We have two boys. They have no idea what their mother likes to do for fun."

Whitney winced, but they shared another quiet laugh.

"So, you don't do what your wife does?"

"Well, my wife is one of those party guests Donna spoke

of who has no limits." He tucked his free hand in his pocket and sipped from an old-fashioned whiskey glass.

"Oh."

What would that be like? Whitney wondered. To come to parties like this with a spouse who had no limits on what sexual acts she would do with other people. Especially if you weren't pumped about the parties to begin with.

"While I've learned to go with the flow and have a good time," he shrugged, "I do have limits."

"And what are they?"

"No whips and chains," he said with a wink. She barked a sharp laugh and looked around to make sure no one heard her. Two women engaged in a big screen kiss at the far end of the path, and though Whitney heard other hushed voices, she saw no one else near them. "I'm kidding." He pulled his hand from his pocket and took her fingers in his. "I'll play, but I'm not really looking for the full sexual experience."

She whooshed a big breath of relief and then embarrassed by her guilelessness, she ducked her head and covered her mouth to hide her laughter.

"First time?"

"Well." She lifted her chin and arched her brows. "The shower."

"Most of the parties are more like this," he told her. "Now and then they do a game night like that."

"Good to know."

"Do you want to marry him?" Evan tugged gently and led her around the second garden. Whitney took another drink and wondered if they were going to walk around all night talking when Shawn might possibly be holed up in a spare bedroom getting his brains sucked out by the redhead she'd seen him with.

Because she didn't trust her voice, she simply nodded.

"He wasn't with you at the shower."

"He was out of town." She stopped walking when they neared a little patio area where four lounge chairs surrounded a firepit. No one was here; they'd walked so far from the house, she wondered if they were still in Frank and Donna's backyard.

Evan set his glass on a small round glass-topped table next to the nearest chair. Whitney noticed it was nearly empty, save for two melting ice cubes and a ring of amber-colored liquid around the bottom. She handed hers over easily when he reached for it, but ropes of nerve tightened in her belly and around her ribcage when he turned to look at her.

"Wanna sit down?" He nodded at the chair.

She needed to sit down. Her knees were a bit weak with something akin to fear, though maybe not so bold and harsh as that. She hesitated, though, because she wasn't sure what he was suggesting or what she was agreeing to by taking one of the lounge chairs.

"C'mon." He reached for her hand and held on while she lowered herself to sit. Her dress skimmed up her thighs a bit as she sat. Evan perched on the end of the chair, Whitney hyper aware of the teeny triangle of peach silk between her legs when their eyes met.

4

"You look like a woman with a lot on her mind."

Sideways on the end of the chair, Evan tipped his head to study her. Whitney tried to laugh, but it was forced, and judging from the grimace on his face, Evan could tell. She let the laugh fade to a sigh as she slumped back in the chair.

"That transparent?" She arched her eyebrows and managed a small smile.

"Sort of." Evan shrugged. In a navy t-shirt, fitted over lean but well-defined shoulders and loose-fitting khaki shorts, he appeared casual but comfortable. He leaned forward and rested his elbows on his knees, his eyes—the blue of a summer sky—watching her closely.

"Um." She frowned, relieved when he shot her a crooked grin. "Sort of transparent?"

"Most people don't just dive into this," he explained. "Now and then, sure. But most people, especially couples, tiptoe in a bit at a time. It's natural to be a bit reluctant."

"Mmm." Lips pressed tightly together, she took a deep

breath through her nose and reached for her glass. "I don't think there's anything natural about any of this."

His easy chuckle made some of the knots of tension in her shoulders and neck ease a bit.

"You're worrying about what he's doing."

"Nope." She shook her head. "I'm not. I'm not thinking about him."

"It's okay."

"How do you—?" She stopped herself. However, Evan and his wife handled this—the parties, the infidelity, the intimacy after the fact—none of that was her business.

"Ask." He lifted a shoulder in a lazy shrug.

Whitney lifted her head when she heard a shriek of laughter and then hushed voices as someone neared them and then faded away again.

"Wouldn't you rather..." She shrugged. "I mean, lots of women here willing to entertain you. You don't have to sit here and babysit me."

"I'm fine," he promised her. "What were you going to ask?"

"How you do this. How you and your wife do this."

Whitney's eyes were drawn to the rise and fall of his shoulders as he took a deep breath.

"It was hard at first," he admitted. "Even for her, and she's the one who wanted to be here."

"Hard how? For her?"

"She wanted the...experiences. The prowling and the chase. The sex. It's..." He pursed his lips as he considered how to explain his thoughts. "It's intense, and it's a thrill. The whole night. You get the invitation, and you just get...cagey... waiting. Wanting. Knowing you're gonna be immersed in skin and liquor and sex."

"Unless you pick a rookie," Whitney interrupted him.

Evan's grin was so big and sweet, it disarmed her. She

watched him as he turned on the chair to face her, his thighs straddling it now. When he scooted forward a bit and reached for her, her body reacted and moved without her permission. But he didn't paw at her. Didn't slide his hands up under her dress. He cupped her chin with gentle fingers and smoothed his thumb over her lip.

Their eyes met, and that uncertainty settled in her stomach again. She wasn't worried that he would force her or hurt her. But what if he forced *the issue* and pushed enough to make her say no? She didn't intend to come back to a party here, but she didn't want to burn any bridges, either.

"Maybe I picked you because you're pretty." He moved his hand just enough to stroke his fingers over her throat. "And maybe looking at pretty women is my thing."

Nervous under his intense gaze, she rolled her lips inward and swallowed hard. He didn't speak, but she recognized the look in his eyes. A kiss. One kiss wouldn't hurt. As if he read her mind, Evan pressed a sweet kiss to her mouth. She closed her eyes and reveled in the press of his warm lips, soft and dry, on hers. His fingers still caressed her neck, teasing a spot under her ear. Whitney reached blindly to put her drink down and then lifted her hand to touch him. She smoothed her fingertips over his face, intrigued by the contrast of his beard stubble over soft skin.

The flick of his tongue over the center of her lips drew a gasp of delight from deep inside. Evan, more skilled at this game than she, dipped the tip of his tongue inside her parted lips. She and Shawn used to kiss like this. The slow, wet kissing that might not lead to anything but more slow, wet kisses. As much as she loved the way Shawn loved her body, she missed this.

She kissed him back, a slow stroke of her tongue over his.

"Janie—my wife—tells me she had three orgasms with

one guy the first time we were here." He sat back, swung his leg over the side of the chair again, and regarded her with a pensive look. "Which…to be honest…was kind of unheard of. For her. For us."

Whitney felt a pang of regret in her belly. She was curious about how a married couple did this stuff, but asking a stranger to share things about his sex life felt wrong. She reached for her glass, and this time, she took a big drink before setting it back on the table.

"That sucked." He glanced at her, shrugged his lips when their eyes met. "Of course, it did. No guy wants to know his wife can come like that but not with him. And in the meantime, I hung out at the bar most of that night. Bronson and I talked NHL and progressive income taxes."

Whitney frowned, but Evan only chuckled.

"Later…like…not quite midnight, I went to the bathroom. I knew Janie was with someone. Thankfully, she still likes closed doors, so I didn't have to sit with a bunch of people and watch my wife have sex with someone else. Not then, anyway." He shook his head. Whitney pressed her lips together to hold back any groans or sighs of commiseration. "A girl followed me. To the bathroom. To be honest with you, it was dark in the hallway. She was younger than me. Blond. Cute, but I didn't really even get a good look at her. Before I knew what was happening—well, I knew what was happening, right?" Evan lifted the corner of his mouth in a guilty grin. "She was on her knees in front of me."

"So, that's how it started? For you?"

He nodded. "Janie and I fought about it for a while. After. Like…weeks. But. Sex got better."

Whitney blinked at him silently, teeth still clamped tight. Evan finally raised his eyebrows and nodded at her, as if demanding she speak.

"Yeah, but sometimes fighting and make up sex is the best kind."

He nodded. "It is. But it was different. Sure, the first time or two after that night, once we finally made it to that, it was rough. Angry. But. Then it was more. For the first time, Janie found her voice. As long as we'd been together, she didn't ask for what she wanted. She didn't…think…outside of what we did, what I did. And all those years, I thought I knew what she liked, what she wanted. Somehow, being with someone new gave her the courage to talk to me. The way she should have been talking to me from the beginning."

Whitney nodded and drew in a deep breath. "And now? Are you angry with her? Do you blame her for…"

"For what?"

"Well. I mean. For this." Whitney nodded her head toward the house. "Does it make you angry that she didn't talk to you before? That it took this for her to open up?"

"No." Evan shook his head. "Not anymore. I regret that I didn't get it when we were younger. And in the beginning of this new phase, yes, I was so angry, I wanted to kill the guy she was with. And then…like I said, things were better. And everything else was still perfect. Every bit of our lives is the same, is better. She's the love of my life. We still go on dates. We went to an ice cream social last weekend at some country church. We were just out driving around. We fly kites. We went skiing last winter. Even made it out of the cabin once to hit the slopes. We parent together. We still fight. But that new intimacy that we found in the bedroom has carried over into every other part of our lives."

Whitney nodded.

"He was on a guys' trip." She licked her lips. "The night of the shower. We had argued not long before that. Before he had to leave. I don't even remember what started the fight—

some girl flirting with him at work, I think, but it snow-balled. So, he decided we should just take a break."

"Which would have been the perfect opportunity for you to have more fun at the shower," Evan pointed out.

"I don't want that," she whispered. "I'm not judging anyone who does. In fact, I'm pretty fascinated, really. But it's not me."

Evan nodded.

"I get it."

"I think he was with someone else." She met Evan's eyes. "In Texas. In fact, I'm pretty sure he was, and it's all I can think about now."

"Did you ask him?"

"Sort of. He reminded me we weren't technically together when he was gone. When I was here for the shower. He said he didn't want to know what I did, and I think that means he doesn't want me to know what he did."

"If he was? Will you forgive him?"

"What's to forgive?" She cleared her throat and dabbed at her eyes. "We weren't together."

"Whitney." Evan tipped his head.

"I don't know. I can't tell you how much that hurts. Thinking that while I was here, miserable...kissing my best friend..." She laughed and hiccupped and wiped at her eyes again. Evan aimed that charming grin at her again. He reached for her, rested his fingers on her ankle. Funny how that innocent touch could comfort her when making love to Shawn and sleeping in his arms didn't.

"It's not even that." She shrugged. "I was twenty-one when we first started seeing each other. I'm twenty-seven. We're dating. Just dating. Six years."

"Biological clock?" Evan stroked his thumb over her ankle bone.

"We're dating. Still. He sleeps over sometimes. He keeps

stuff at my house. I have stuff at his place. It's not enough. For me. It's not even just the biological clock. I have time for that. I know I do. I just want more from him. For us."

"I think after six years you have the right to ask that of him."

She rolled her lips inward again and managed a smile.

"Tell me you don't counsel rookies at every party," she said with a laugh. She stretched and looked around. The sky was colored with evening shadows now; the purples and pinks of the sunset hanging low behind them. Whitney could hear the techno beat of the music from the house. If she listened closely, she could hear hushed voices somewhere nearby.

"I don't." He shook his head. "Don't feel sorry for me, Whitney. You lose your inhibitions after a while. This might have been Janie's thing, but I could stay home if I wanted to."

Whitney grinned and pushed her hair back from her face.

"Wow." She nodded. "Okay."

"Do you want another drink?"

"I could go hang out with Bronson for a while, if you wanna cruise the scene."

Evan chuckled. "I'm good."

"I don't think I need another drink," she said softly. "But thank you for asking."

"Feel any better?" He tilted his head and looked at her hopefully.

Whitney started to answer, to lie and say yes, but when he tipped his head at her knowingly, she laughed and tossed her hands up helplessly.

"Not really but thank you for...sharing...your experience with me."

"You're welcome." He nodded. "You have to know I'm selfishly wishing you would come back and decide to tiptoe in and test the water."

Whitney gaped at him silently, her face on fire.

"I hope that doesn't offend you."

"No." She shook her head. "I'm not offended. Just…"

"You're very pretty, and if all I can send you home with is words, I'm gonna do it right. I don't know what your guy is doing right now, but I would love to lay you back in that chair and make love to you."

He was attractive. The silver in his hair was sexy, the grin he wore now almost lethal. If she weren't in love with Shawn Green, if she were single and here with a friend, would she take him up on his offer? Would she have the nerve to spread her legs for a stranger, the way Leslie had done a few weeks ago?

"The first thing I would do is slide those straps over your shoulders and look at you. I'm guessing you have beautiful breasts."

"How long did it take you to be able to look a stranger in the eye and say that?"

"A while," he admitted, grin dialed back to insolent and sexy. "I'll stop if I'm making you uncomfortable."

Whitney ducked her head and tugged at her lower lip with her teeth.

"You're fair skinned, so I think your nipples are strawberry pink. Imagine me licking a little cream from each of them."

Whitney snorted and dropped her head back to rest on the chair.

"Uncle." She held her hands up and closed her eyes. "It's too much. If I weren't in love with someone else, I would find you crazy attractive. And that's about the craziest, boldest thing I can say to you. I'm sorry."

"It's okay," he promised her. "Let's walk. The yard is awesome." Evan climbed to his feet with ease and then offered his hand to help her up. Whitney took it, even linked her fingers with his as he handed her the martini. "Just remember what kind of party this is. You're gonna see a lot between here and wherever we end up."

"I'm not a prude," she argued weakly. "I just can't do it. Not now."

Evan let go of her hand, but before Whitney could miss his easy touch, he threw a casual arm around her back and squeezed her arm.

"Are you gonna demand more? Give him an ultimatum?"

"I don't know." She shrugged, even though that had been exactly her plan when she and Shawn had arrived earlier. Now she wondered if she should be satisfied with what they had. Could she really go back to dating again? Someone new? She was only twenty-seven, but still. Whitney certainly wasn't cut out for this kind of thing. She didn't love the idea of random hook ups anywhere. If she cut Shawn loose, she'd be starting over. Alone.

"If you do, and he walks, meet me back here."

Grateful for the teasing tone, Whitney laughed and shook her head. They walked together through the yard, several areas enclosed by copses of trees like the one they'd just left. Whitney marveled not only at the size of the yard, but at the trees and plants that created cozy, private pockets everywhere. It was almost as if the yard had been designed for sexy, clandestine things.

She wasn't a prude, but she was glad Evan had reminded her that the entire backyard was fair game for the couples at the party. What she didn't see—and they did pass a few couples, nude bodies entangled in intriguing positions—she heard. Evan talked nonsense—she caught something about a news story about an alligator on a golf course in Florida— but she knew he was hoping to distract her. From the scenery, maybe. More likely, from her fears about Shawn.

When they reached the bar, Whitney was so happy to see

Bronson—fully clothed, smile on his face, talking to Frank—that she overlooked a couple messing around by the pool. Evan and Bronson exchanged a few words, and Whitney exchanged her empty martini glass for water. Evan set his glass on the bar and turned to her.

"You want me to stick around?"

"No." She shook her head and offered him a sad smile. "I'm fine."

"Because I could bore you to sleep with more news stories," he offered.

Moved by his kindness—and a little bit flattered by his interest—Whitney stepped closer to him and slipped her arms around his shoulders.

"Thank you." She hugged him hard, ignoring his erection pressed into her middle. The flash of guilt she had for leading him on—had she?—made her linger there a moment longer. Evan closed his arms around her and kissed her forehead.

"You know what?" He tipped his head to study her, his smile warm and tender. Over his shoulder, Frank and Bronson still talked, neither of them paying them a bit of attention. "Any time you wanna come back? And take a walk? Talk a bit? You find me."

Heat flushed her cheeks again. The weight of her emotions rested on her shoulders, so hard and so heavy, for just a moment, she was glad Evan was holding her up. She shouldn't have come. Because she had no interest in a free pass to cheat on Shawn. And now she felt bad for wasting Evan's time when he'd been so patient and kind.

"Thanks." She grinned and nodded. Evan dropped a quick, familiar peck on her lips and then he was gone. Whitney turned back to the bar to pick up her water and locked eyes with Shawn. Elbow on the bar, left hand in his hip pocket, he watched her with cool indifference.

5

He looked decidedly casual, propped there at the bar. Eyes never leaving hers, he took his hand from his pocket and reached for the beer near his elbow. Paralyzed with guilt and unease, Whitney eyed him curiously. When they were together, post-orgasm, Shawn was laid back and easy going. While he looked casual, she wasn't sure he had the same loose, boneless appearance at the moment.

What hurt, though, was that he didn't look angry. Or jealous. Or worried, even. Didn't look like he cared at all that some other man had just walked her up to the bar and hugged and kissed her. That she might have done something intimate with that other man. Aware that they weren't alone, she sipped her water, capped the bottle, and then turned to walk away from him. She was ready to go. She wouldn't get far without keys, but she couldn't stand here in this stare off with him, either.

The techno beat of the party music thudded in her breastbone when she went inside. Still a bit stung over Shawn's nonreaction to Evan kissing her goodbye, she averted her gaze from a couple on the loveseat facing the French door.

Even so, she catalogued flat breasts and big round nipples and a guy kneeling on the floor between her legs. The last thing Whitney wanted to see now, anyone in an intimate situation. Well, maybe the second to last thing. She had no desire to look at Shawn again and watch him look at her like she was a stranger.

She remembered from the last time she was here that there was a small powder room down the hall by the mud room. Afraid she would lose it now, afraid those damned tears would fall, she made her way through the kitchen toward that hall. Careful not to rush, to appear flustered, she held her head high until she was alone in the hall. The music still pounded through her body, but at least here the scenery was better. A glimpse at a high-tech washer and dryer. A pair of garden clogs tucked under a wooden bench. A framed poster—looked like an old family picture—on the wall across from the powder room.

Much to her relief, the door was unlocked. She pulled in a deep breath and nearly shuddered with pent-up emotion as she stepped inside. She flipped the light on. Someone tugged at the door behind her, and she caught movement in the mirror, but suddenly the room went dark, and someone pressed into the small space with her. The door closed, drowning out the music, the click of the lock like a gunshot in the tiny room.

Unafraid—she'd been intimately involved with him for six years, so she knew him by his scent, by the feel of his body near hers—but startled nonetheless, she gasped in surprise when he spun her around to press her back to his chest and clamped his hand over her mouth.

His cock like steel at her back, he dipped his head to rest his chin in her hair. Whitney twisted and yanked her face from his grasp and struggled to catch her breath. He settled his hands on her hips, digging his fingers in possessively. He tilted his hips, rubbed his hard-on over her and then pressed hard into her ass, drawing a reluctant moan up from low in her belly.

"What the fuck is this?" His voice was low and tight with barely controlled fury. Whitney reached for the wall, the water bottle slipping from her hand as she pressed her hands up for balance. Neither of them reacted to the thwack of the bottle on the floor.

Hands still heavy on her hips, he leaned to bite her, teeth clenching hard enough on her neck to hurt. Her nipples tightened, and wet heat pooled between her legs. The things Evan had said to her earlier—about licking cream from her breasts—had stirred them, her to life, but Shawn's fury awakened a desperate need inside her.

Disoriented in the dark, in someone else's house, Whitney squeezed her eyes closed. Shawn moved suddenly; she cried out when his hard body was no longer pressed up against hers.

"Shawn."

And then he was back, his hands on her ankles, the heat of his breath on the back of first one knee and then the other. She'd expected him to grind on her, his cock against her hips, her ass. Instead, the flick of his tongue at her inner thighs made her whimper with delight.

He pushed her dress up, and Whitney reached with one hand to hold it and give him access to her body. She wanted his hands on her, not her clothing. But rather than touch her, rather than sink his fingers into her wet folds, he dragged them back down her legs and licked her ass cheek.

"Shawn."

He bit her again, his teeth closing hard over her flesh. She yelped and jumped away from him. Hands near her feet, he linked his fingers around her ankles and teased her with his tongue over the curve of her ass cheeks and down her thighs.

He nipped again at the backs of her knees, making her tremble and sag against the wall. In the darkness, she opened her eyes and listened to him breathe.

"This." He moved again. Fingers wrapped around her outer thighs, he pressed his thumbs into her folds and spread her wide open. Whitney moaned at the exposure, the air on her wet, sensitive skin. "This is mine."

She surrendered when he licked her, the flat of his tongue dragging from her clit and back over her folds and finally over her ass.

"Shawn, please" she whispered, desperate for his mouth there again. For the slide of his wet heat over hers, for the pressure, the friction on her clit. Instead, he thrust his fingers inside her and worked her ass cheek with his teeth. Fingers pumping and sliding in the age-old sex act, he withheld the final stroke, denying her the release she needed. She cried out in protest again when he moved, his clothed body dragging up against her when he stood.

She heard the rasp of his zipper and the rustle of clothes as he shoved his shorts out of his way. Whitney had the fleeting thought, fear, that he might have been with someone else tonight as he grabbed her by the hips, tugged the thong to the side, and drove his cock deep and hard inside her.

"I love you," she whispered, but she wasn't sure he heard her as he labored behind her, panting and groaning with each thrust of his hips. Heat, like lightning, shook and burned in her core. She chanted his name, begged for more, for his fingers between her legs, for release, and finally, desperation won out and she slumped forward, left arm pressed to the wall and slipped her fingers under the thong to touch herself.

Shawn covered her hand with his, and the knot of tension inside her exploded immediately.

"Mine," he repeated, as he clamped his hands on her hips

again and held her while he moved faster and harder behind her. She trembled, her body quaking with aftershocks when Shawn came with a feral, possessive growl.

He pulled away from her, leaving her thighs sticky with his cum. Again, she wondered if he'd been with anyone before following her into the bathroom. She was glad for the dark now as tears trickled over her cheeks. He might never commit to marrying her, whether he loved her or wanted her because it was more convenient to stay rather than break up, but he wouldn't do that. He wouldn't fuck a stranger at a party and then come to her and put his cock inside her just hours later. Would he?

She sobbed and ducked her head when he flipped the light on.

"What?" He sounded irritated as he plucked several tissues from a box on the small sink.

"I need a minute."

"Why?"

From the corner of her eye, she saw his deep, dramatic shrug.

"We've been fucking for six years, Whitney. I've watched you clean yourself up before."

Mouth dry, she tried to swallow. In light of how they'd just been together, maybe the term fit. But his casual term for their intimacy hurt. She took the tissues he offered and lifted her dress with trembling hands to wipe at the remains of their fun on her inner thighs. He had shoved her thong to the side when he drove into her, and now she was hyperaware of the uncomfortably tight, pulling sensation between her ass cheeks. Under his intense eyes, she wiggled out of it. She intended to toss it in the small trash can between the sink and the toilet, but Shawn took it and tucked it in his pocket.

"Why are you crying?" he asked as he dabbed at the tip of his cock with a tissue. He glanced at her as he tossed it in the toilet and then pulled his shorts up and zipped and buttoned them.

"Can we just go?"

"Your party," he reminded her in a cool, clipped tone.

She turned to the oval mirror over the sink and dabbed at the smeared mascara under her eyes. She'd never make it look good, but after a few moments, she decided it was as good as it would get and washed her hands. Shawn followed her out. She'd forgotten Frank and Donna had each guest take a breathalyzer as they left, so she didn't get a chance to warn Shawn as they walked back through the hall and to the main entry of the house. She smacked into Shawn's backside when he pulled up short and ducked her head into his shoulder when she saw Frank there by the door. She'd touched up her makeup, but that didn't mean she could hide that she'd been crying just moments ago.

"Hey." Frank greeted Shawn in that big, booming voice. Whitney took a deep breath, but she lifted her head when she felt Shawn move. He shook Frank's hand again, but Whitney tuned out the guy talk. She figured that Shawn might gripe about the breathalyzer later, but he didn't argue with Frank about taking it. Since Shawn was under the legal limit—Whitney heard Frank say something about seeing Shawn drink only two beers—and he was holding the keys, Frank didn't even bother with Whitney. Instead, he drew her in for a quick hug, and then finally—and all too soon, at the same time—she and Shawn were back outside in front of the house, heading back to his car. Hands tucked in his pockets, he didn't even glance at her as they walked.

The ride home was uncomfortably quiet. Whitney had no idea what Shawn was thinking, but she decided the night had been a disaster. She was no closer to having any promises of a forever future with him, and now she had to wonder if he'd fooled around with someone tonight, besides worrying about his *awesome!! night* in Texas.

And still, she kept coming back to the thought that if she didn't trust him, they had no future. If she wasted any more time in the relationship, it was on her. He pulled into her driveway, but when he put the car in park, he left it running.

He wasn't coming in.

The truth hit her hard, ripped through her chest, and left her breathless.

"I'll walk you in." He finally broke the silence. She wanted to argue, but the knife in her throat made it impossible to speak. She flicked her gaze up to his and then to his hand when he turned the key in the ignition. The engine cut out, but he left the keys hanging as he climbed out of the car.

"I'll call you tomorrow, Whit—"

She shook her head slightly and turned away from him. On the small front porch, her steady hands unlocked the door. Finally, she turned to look up at him.

"I think it's just best for both of us to walk away, Shawn."

As if she'd rehearsed it, as if she was ready, her voice was cool and steady. Inside, the ache of missing him was already big enough to swallow her and make her invisible to him. But she wouldn't cry again.

"What does that mean?" He groaned and ran his fingers back through his hair. "We just did this a few weeks ago, Whitney. What's the point? We're too old for this."

"We are," she whispered and nodded in agreement. "I love you, but I can't do this anymore."

"Do what?" he argued.

Whitney blinked at the threat of tears. This was a recurring argument, and the fact that each time, Shawn had to make it new, had to pretend that he didn't understand why she was upset only made it worse. She saw it now, the way he played her to put her off. To wear her down.

"If you love me." She touched his lips, her fingers searching for goodbye there on his mouth. "You'll let me go."

He didn't argue, and as she stood on her tiptoes to kiss him and then turned her back to him to go inside, his silence hurt more than any angry words he could have thrown at her.

6

Whitney's house could probably fit inside Donna and Frank's at least three times. The entire lot her place was built on would probably fit inside their house. But she didn't care. She loved the cute little house she'd snatched up two years ago. She'd grown tired of apartment living and fallen in love with the nearly new place at first sight. She had been confident enough in her job to apply for a home loan, and she'd secretly believed within a few years, she and Shawn would be married and living there together.

"So." Leslie topped her glass off and then leaned over the small patio table to pour Whitney more wine. "Tell me again."

"Tell you what again?" Whitney sighed. "I've told you everything." Rather than look at her friend, she studied her feet, propped and crossed on the chair next to her.

"You went to the party. And when he brought you home, you broke up."

"Yeah." Whitney nodded. "That's about it."

"That's not it," Leslie argued. "I wanna know the details of the damned party, but first I'm being selfless here and asking about you. What the hell happened with Shawn?"

Whitney laughed softly. "So selfless."

"Why did he break it off this time?"

"He didn't," Whitney answered. Eyes on the remains of the salad she'd eaten for dinner, she watched Leslie snitch a slice of carrot. Leslie had eaten every last bite of her chicken club sandwich, but apparently, she was still hungry. After Whitney had blown her off with simple texts this morning and accidentally on purpose missed three phone calls this afternoon, Leslie had shown up at her door an hour ago with takeout and demanded to know what the hell was going on.

"He—?" Leslie popped the carrot slice in her mouth and chewed slowly, intense eyes lethal on Whitney. "What?"

"I can't do it anymore, Leslie," Whitney mumbled. "I want more than dating. Than sleepover sex. Than watching him play golf with friends. I thought by now we would be married. That we would have babies together, and that he could pass on his love of golf or baseball to our son. That instead of morning sex and him going back to his place, he would get up and mow our yard or fix our sink or wash our car."

The empathy in Leslie's gaze burned Whitney. Her friend was in the beginning of a relationship that already seemed more promising than the one Whitney had been slogging through for years.

"And instead, we have completely separate lives. And what makes it worse." Whitney drew a deep breath and then shook her head.

"What?" Leslie tipped her head and nodded to coax it out of her.

"Every time I ask for more, every time this argument comes up, he pushes reset and we start over. Like it's not important enough to remember. Or maybe, like he's trying to hammer it in my brain that it's not important enough to him to remember why I'm upset."

After Shawn left last night, she'd showered and dressed in pjs and then parked in front of her TV. Empty and numb, she'd watched two hours of infomercials before she even realized they were infomercials. Once in bed, she'd tossed and turned. Her mind raced with memories of her and Shawn, mostly good things, and then it slowed and offered her the dreams she'd had for the two of them back when she'd first fallen in love with him.

She hadn't cried, and she didn't cry now. She was exhausted, weary of the heartache that now lingered even in her happiest days.

"Aren't you going to say something?" she finally asked when Leslie remained silent and the compressor on the central air conditioning unit stopped suddenly, leaving the small backyard in a hush.

"You deserve more," Leslie said softly, "but that doesn't mean searching for more isn't going to hurt."

"I need to get his stuff back to him. Get him out of here. His memory."

"You could call a priest," Leslie suggested.

Whitney laughed softly and shook her head. "I want him to be happy. And I know being tied down to me isn't what he wants."

"'kay," Leslie nodded, "but as your best friend, I reserve the right to say mean things about him for a while."

"We had sex at the party."

Leslie, glass at her lips, paused and stared at Whitney over the rim. "I'm—what? With each other?"

"Yeah." Whitney sighed. "I went to the bathroom. He followed me in. He was pissed. So, we had rough, pissed-off, against-the-wall sex."

"And?"

"It was incredible," Whitney admitted. "But it was cold. And empty. And I hate that we're gonna end it on that note. I won't be Whitney, someone he loved for a few years. I'll be the girl he fucked against the wall at a sex party and then dumped."

"You broke up with him," Leslie reminded her.

"You think he would admit that to the next piece of ass?"

"Don't." Leslie shook her head. "Look, whatever his hang ups with commitment, I do think he loves you. Don't belittle what you guys had."

Whitney sucked in a quick breath and nodded. Leslie was right. She had to believe she and Shawn had shared something special, but they wanted different things from a relationship and from life. No one's fault. Time to move on.

"Thank you," she whispered.

"But." Leslie tipped her head. When she didn't continue, Whitney snuck a peek at her and watched her nibble on her lower lip, lost in thought.

"What?"

"What did he say? I mean. You had incredible sex, and a short drive later, you say thanks, see ya? What happened, Whit?"

"I'm still wondering what he did in Texas," Whitney mumbled. "And I shouldn't. Because we weren't together at the time, so it's his business."

"I disagree with that," Leslie interrupted her. She shrugged her eyebrows when Whitney shot her a frown.

"And then last night…" Whitney sighed. "I don't know what he did. But he was at the bar with Bronson when Evan and I walked up. He watched Evan kiss me goodbye. Just stood there staring at me like he didn't even know me."

Leslie fixed her with a hard, curious stare. Whitney knew she was dying to ask about Evan, but she wouldn't. Leslie was too generous, always had been. She'd wait until Whitney told her about Shawn and then she might ask about a guy who kissed her goodbye.

"I was upset. So, I went back inside. To the little powder room by the back door. He followed me in. Flipped my dress up, and it was over in less than five minutes."

"Did he seal the deal for you?"

"I did," Whitney mumbled.

"And then what?"

Whitney laughed. "We left. Frank had him blow, and then we left. He didn't talk. Well, I mean when we were doing it, but on the drive home—"

"What did he say? When you were having sex?"

Whitney stared at Leslie, her mouth agape.

"Well. I mean. I wouldn't normally ask, but this is different," Leslie said defensively.

"He put his hands on me. And he said I was his."

"So, he was pissed."

"I don't think he liked the party," Whitney admitted. "He asked me what the fuck it was about. He was suspicious before everything got started."

"That says something, doesn't it?"

"It might say he likes to fuck me and doesn't want to share, but it doesn't say let's get married and start a family."

Leslie cringed and nodded. "You're right. I'm sorry."

"Neither of us spoke. On the drive home. He walked me up to the door, but he left his keys in the car. He had no plans to stay."

"Maybe he just wanted to process the night."

"When I told him I thought we just needed to let go and walk away, he was angry. Said we're too old to keep doing this. I agreed. But then he acted like he didn't get where I was going. That I haven't said before that I want more for us. And he left without much of a fight at all."

Leslie chewed on her lip again. Whitney watched her sip her wine.

"What?"

"What what?" Leslie met her eyes and shook her head.

"Just say it."

"Nothing to say."

"I've known you longer than I knew Shawn. I know you're holding back."

Leslie groaned. "I don't know, Whit. I just...what if you rushed into this? What if you're just stung about Texas, and so you rushed into a break up?"

"Rushed—?" Whitney snapped. She watched Leslie climb to her feet and pace a circle around the table. "Six years, Leslie. I've given him six years."

"I know. But you've only really talked to him about what you want a few times. What if he just wasn't ready? What if he's the one?"

"Who the hell are you? And where's my friend?" Whitney pushed her hair back from her face. "Les, you wouldn't have given him six years to commit."

"I know." Leslie stopped and stood behind Whitney. She dropped her hands on Whitney's shoulders and squeezed. "Whit, I love you. If you want me to call and schedule a moving truck to come and pack Shawn's clothes and toothbrush, they'll be here Monday. You want a priest here to exorcise his soul? I'll have one here tomorrow after mass. I'm just...You and I are made differently. I wouldn't have put up with him for years. But that doesn't make it wrong that you did. You love him. I just want you to be happy, and I'm not sure life without Shawn will make you happy."

"But don't I deserve the chance to see? If I can live without him?" Whitney swallowed hard, but the words were still small and breathless.

Leslie squeezed her shoulders again. She leaned over and rested her forehead on the top of Whitney's head.

"Absolutely. And I'll be here with you every day you need me. Just know that if you still love him, if you can't be happy without him, know I'm not gonna judge you for that. Okay?'

Whitney nodded.

"Okay?" Leslie said again.

"Okay." Whitney covered Leslie's hand on her right shoulder and patted her. "Okay."

"Okay, now. Tell me who the hell Evan is and what you did at the party."

Whitney snorted and rolled her eyes. Leslie moved; she plopped down in her chair again and stared at Whitney with bold curiosity.

"Well, he's married," Whitney began. Leslie closed her eyes and shook her head, but when she opened them again, she smiled and nodded. "He was one of the guys from *Spin the Bottle*."

"Yeah?"

"Little bit older. Some gray in his hair. Sliver-rimmed glasses."

"Yeah." Leslie nodded. "Okay. Wow. Really?"

"I didn't have sex with him," Whitney argued.

"But what? What'd you do? How did this party go?"

"Mm." Whitney took a drink and licked her lips. "Everybody got a passport. And on the back, they were stamped with puzzle pieces. You had to find someone with a puzzle piece that would interlock with yours."

"And Shawn's didn't?"

"Of course not. I wonder if Donna did that on purpose."

Leslie raised her eyebrows but said nothing.

"So. Evan and I took a walk. Just…through the backyard. He held my hand. We talked a lot."

"Tell me you did more than talk to the guy? I mean, okay, you didn't have sex. But you left here looking smokin' hot."

Whitney laughed softly. "I asked him a lot of questions. About how he and his wife handle the parties. The infidelity. Because I don't think I could do it. Well, I didn't. Did I? Evan kissed me. And he made it clear that he was interested. And told me to look for him if I ever went back to a party like that. But nothing happened."

"Did Shawn see any of that?"

"I don't know." Whitney shook her head. "He was talking to someone at the kitchen island when Evan and I went outside. So I don't know what he saw. What he thinks. What he did. I have no idea."

"And you don't want to know?"

"Clean break. It's the only way I can deal with breaking up. If he tells me he saw me with Evan, that he saw me holding hands with him, I'll feel guilty. If he tells me the girl he was with gave him a blowjob, it'll break my heart. If he tells me nothing happened, I'm not sure I'll believe him. And that's a problem, Leslie. If he doesn't want to commit to me, in my head that translates to I'm not enough. And if I don't trust him, then we have no future."

Leslie sighed and finally answered with a slow nod.

"Okay. I get it." She nodded. "You could go back to a party. And have some fun."

"Are you kidding me?"

"Why not?"

"Um. Because I'm not into hook ups with strangers."

Leslie snorted, and then when Whitney remembered her friend had done just that and her face flooded with heat, Leslie threw her head back and laughed.

"Well, maybe you should be," Leslie said with an exaggerated shrug. "I highly recommend it."

"I'm not looking for something new," Whitney argued softly. "I just need some time to focus on me."

"And what better way to do that than a party at Donna and Frank's house? It's safe. No strings attached. And you might find someone else to focus on you."

Whitney rolled her eyes. "What would Shawn think?"

"Shawn doesn't get to think anything anymore. Remember? You could go to the next party and find a guy and have a drink and do nothing. Or you could go skinny dipping."

"Nope." Whitney shook her head. "Nope. Not happening. How's Asher?"

There was no mistaking the way Leslie's face lit up at the mention of her boyfriend's name.

"Good." She nodded. "He asked me to go to Chicago with him next weekend. He wants to see his dad. And we're gonna do a night in the city."

"Do a night in the city? Or do each other at night in the city?"

"Yes." Leslie grinned and winked.

"I'm going to join a yoga class," Whitney decided. "And maybe a book group."

Leslie studied her silently for a moment and finally tipped her head. "How about a cat? Gonna get one of those? Pick up knitting?"

"Shut up!" Whitney laughed and lunged forward to take a swing at Leslie.

"Okay. Yoga is okay. You have my blessing to do that. But if you're doing a book group, make it one that reads sexy books. Not devotional stuff."

"I don't need to read sexy stuff when I'm sleeping alone."

"You have a vibrator," Leslie reminded her. "And you have friends that throw really interesting parties."

"Oh my God." Whitney rolled her eyes. "Okay. I'll go if you go."

"You're kidding, right?" Leslie drained her glass and set it on the table with a loud clack. "You think I'd share Asher Collins? Not a chance in hell."

"But you can go and not participate," Whitney reminded her. "Remember? Go and have a drink with Asher. Talk to Bronson."

"And having me and Asher at the bar is gonna give you the guts to go down on someone in the spare bedroom?"

"Oh, hell no. If I ever go back? I'm looking for a guy like Asher."

"Broad shoulders and a ponytail?"

"No. A guy who likes to give."

7

Whitney considered herself in shape, but in truth, she wasn't. All the on again and off again exercising left her somewhere in the dangerous zone of thinking she was athletic and fit and pushing herself too hard and risking injury. So far, she hadn't actually hurt herself, but she spent the first few weeks of being single with sore muscles. The first day or two were particularly bad; she felt a bit like she'd been hit by a train. She ran—or started out on a run the first day and ended up walking—and she rode her bike through a city park near her home. She found a yoga class and learned quickly that she wasn't as limber as she thought and that she had some balance issues.

In all aspects of her life, apparently.

She missed Shawn so much that it was a physical ache in the pit of her stomach. She'd packed his stuff up—two boxes of shirts and shoes and soaps and toothbrushes—immediately, but two weeks later, the boxes were still on the floor in her bedroom. She'd caved on day six and pulled one of his shirts from one of the boxes and put it on. Whenever she was at home now, she wore it. If she had to take it off to wash it, she found herself topless, sprawled out across her bed, waiting for the washer and dryer to hurry up and get it finished. She could wear a different shirt, but she reasoned that no one needed her and who the hell cared if she was topless while she did laundry. And if Shawn ever came by to get his stuff, he was less likely to notice one shirt missing than if she started wearing another and then another.

He didn't come to get his stuff. Not even after she texted him and he answered and said he would. Each time she laid eyes on the boxes, she found herself irritated with him. But she didn't go and get her stuff from his place, either. For one thing, she didn't even know what was there. The only thing she wanted from his place was him. And she also liked the idea that if he was entertaining women at his apartment, they might possibly find her stuff and think he was still with her.

She kind of hated that she'd sunk so low to play the mind games, but on the other hand, Shawn had belonged to her for six years. She hated the idea of other women loving him. She saw him once. At the grocery store. He was pulling out of the parking lot as she turned in. He'd honked and waved at her, and then she had stupidly sat in her car in the lot for a few minutes wondering if he would double back to say hi. After all, he had honked at her. As if nothing had happened. He had honked and waved at her as if they were friends, when Whitney's heart had dropped to that yawning pit in her belly when she saw him.

He didn't double back to say hi. He didn't text.

Leslie kept her busy. She dragged her to ball games, at least a few a week. Leslie's boss had almost enough grandchildren to field a whole baseball team, so there was always a game to watch. Whitney didn't love going, but it beat sitting at home and wondering what Shawn was doing.

She bumped into Frank at the bank often, but of course, they didn't talk about the parties. The number one rule for the parties was discretion, so no one at the bank even whispered or mumbled about what might have happened at this party or that. Whitney assumed that if Frank didn't know the party had been a disaster for her and Shawn, then Donna didn't know, either.

Donna dropped in now and then at the bank to bring Frank's lunch. Whitney's cubicle wasn't near Frank's, so no matter what sort of treats Donna might have delivered, it didn't matter to Whitney.

She joined a book club, and then when she realized it was the same club Jace Hardin's wife, Erin, was in, she made Leslie go, too. The Hardins owned the landscaping business where Leslie worked; Whitney, Leslie, and Jace had gone to school together. The first book they read after she and Leslie joined was a sweeping historical novel about the second world war. Whitney loved it; Leslie tolerated it.

Donna delivered another invitation to Whitney at the bank. This one was grey, rather than crème, and it had only Whitney's name on the envelope. So, Whitney assumed either the grapevine at work had delivered the news of her break up to Frank—her break up technically had nothing to do with the parties, so it was fair game—or Leslie had mentioned it to Asher who told Donna, his aunt.

No matter. She had no intention of going to the party. She'd eaten the cupcake Donna delivered with the invitation and stuck the envelope in her book that she kept in her purse for lunch time entertainment. When Leslie—hanging out at her house—found the envelope later that evening, Whitney snatched it away from her immediately.

"I know what it is," Leslie reminded her.

"Great." Whitney shrugged. "Not going."

"I talked to Asher about it."

"About what exactly?" Whitney set the envelope on her

counter and kept her eye on Leslie, who was sprawled on the couch.

"Going to one of the parties."

"You want to?"

"No." Leslie sighed and rubbed her face with her hands. "For you."

Whitney chugged a big drink of water and then swiped the back of her hand over her mouth. She'd gone for a run— okay, she'd worked herself up from a walk to a jog, at least— and come home to find Leslie on the porch, waiting for her. Maybe she couldn't move fast, but she'd jogged a few miles, and the humidity made it feel like she'd slogged through a tropical jungle rather than city streets. She wanted a shower. A salad. Maybe a glass of wine.

Not this.

Sure, she was always happy to see her best friend, but she didn't want to talk about the parties. Even though she knew better, she associated the break up with what happened at the party she and Shawn had gone to. True. She'd decided before going that she was doing it only to test him—which was wrong of her—and she'd decided to end it after the party, regardless, unless maybe he'd gone down on a knee to propose to her. But in her head, it was all jumbled together, and she didn't like thinking about it.

"So. You talked to Asher about going to a sex party for your pathetic, loser best friend."

"Yep." Leslie nodded.

Whitney laughed and then groaned, frustrated with her friend for trying to push things on her that she didn't want. She set her glass on the counter and then perched on the opposite arm of the couch.

"Is he on board? Maybe we could do a threesome. Better yet, we could stay home and spoon. Can three people spoon?"

"He said he would totally go sit at the bar with me and talk to Bronson if you wanna go and need moral support."

"What?" Whitney screeched. "You told him I *want* to go? But I need moral support?"

"Well, no. But I mentioned it. And I said that you *should* go. And he said he would go."

"Not going."

"When's the party?"

"I dunno. Didn't open the invite."

"So, open it." Leslie climbed off the couch.

"No."

"I talked to Shawn last night," Leslie told her.

"Wait." Whitney put her hand up to stop Leslie. "What?"

"I happen to know that the party is next weekend. Because Donna told me."

Whitney huffed out an irritated sigh and combed her hair back from her face.

"Oh my God. Please stop. I love you but stop. You guys are my friends. Stop sitting around and pow-wowing about me behind my back. Do I look like I'm struggling? Am I acting dark and depressed?"

"Well, no, but—"

"No. I'm not. I'm fine. I don't appreciate that you're making plans for me—"

"First of all, we're not. Asher and I had dinner with Donna and Frank two nights ago. We went for pizza. Everyone kept their clothes on. It was a lot like anyone else going for pizza. They wanted to check in with Asher to see how his dad's doing."

Whitney stared silently at Leslie, still a bit angry and now a little guilt-stricken for not considering that Leslie and Asher might be with Donna and Frank for family reasons. Things that had nothing to do with Whitney.

"And second, Whit, I know you're fine. You're killing it.

You're making me think I need to join your yoga class. You've memorized the batting order for all of Jace's nieces' and nephews' ball games. You're an overachiever in book club. I mean, you had three pages of notes on the first book. And you have two more books in your bedroom, just waiting."

"And that's bad? Me? Filling my time and staying busy? That's bad?" Whitney picked at her nails, refusing to meet Leslie's eyes.

"It's good," Leslie admitted. "But I know you. And I know that even if you are enjoying the new things you're doing, you're trying to fill the spot that Shawn left. You're trying to replace him."

"Isn't that what you're supposed to do? After a break up? Move on?"

"But you still love him."

Whitney blinked and finally lifted her head to meet Leslie's gaze. "Well, it's kind of hard to just stop loving someone, Leslie. I'm doing my best. But it'll take some time."

"But you *don't have to* stop loving him."

Whitney stared at Leslie, waiting for her to continue.

"I saw him."

"Don't tell me he told you he's still in love with me." Whitney shook her head. "Don't lie to me, Leslie. I trust you not to lie to me."

"He didn't say that. But he doesn't look any happier than you do."

"Where did you see him?"

"Asher and I were at Keely's game," Leslie told her. Keely was the oldest Hardin granddaughter, so her games were competitive and exciting. But it made no sense for Shawn to be there. Unless he was with someone.

"And?" Whitney shrugged.

"He was on the tennis courts by the field," Leslie continued. "I saw him pull up. So, I went over to talk to him for a minute."

"Who was he playing with?" Whitney assumed it would be a woman; she even considered some of the women Shawn worked with, including the intern that had caused the fight that led to the break up right before he left for Texas.

"Jeff Demarco."

"Oh."

Jeff Demarco was one of Shawn's bosses at the computer sales and repairs office where he worked. Fifty-four, married for thirty years, and four kids. Didn't sound like Shawn had been out flirting last night.

"I waited until he was done. Until Jeff left. I watched him. Shawn just sat on the bleachers for a long time. You know? The bleachers by the courts, so I could see him from the ball diamond. I finally walked over to talk to him. He looked exhausted."

"I'm sure he was if he'd just played tennis," Whitney mumbled. "Jeff's an athlete. He probably mopped the floor with Shawn's ass. I'd be tired—"

"Shut up." Leslie shook her head. "I don't mean like that. He said he misses you."

"Remember a few minutes ago? When I said I trust you?"

"I'm not lying. No, he didn't say he was wildly in love with you and was considering throwing himself off a bridge if you didn't call him. But he said he misses you."

Whitney swallowed hard and tried to summon her courage to ask more questions.

"Did he say anything else?"

"He said you shocked the hell out of him. Breaking up with him like that."

"What? Because we'd never talked about it before?" Whitney rolled her eyes and climbed to her feet. She turned her back to Leslie and crossed the kitchen to open the fridge.

"No, but because you were so calm. And cool. Like you'd practiced it, and there was no talking you out of it."

"Yeah? Well, he didn't even try."

"He was upset about the party."

Whitney turned to stare at Leslie, but when her friend didn't say more, she swung the refrigerator door closed and then moved back to the living room to lean on the couch.

"What do you mean? What did he say?"

"He didn't. Not really. He said he was floored by what he'd seen. And he was reeling from that on the drive home. Trying to figure out what he thought. And then you told him you wanted to break up."

"I told him I thought it was best to walk away."

"Which means you wanted to break up," Leslie said with a nod. "You walked away from him with another guy."

"And nothing happened. You know nothing happened, Leslie. You told him that. Right?"

"No, Whit, I didn't. Because he didn't go into what bothered him about the party. I sure wasn't going to bring it up."

Whitney's heart pounded in her throat and her ears. She felt the crazy, racing beat in her fingertips, and her belly twisted with nerves.

"You know what?" She shook her head. "No. Just no. You suggested I go to the party and let Shawn wonder what I was doing. He didn't even ask. And no. Because we've been doing this for way too damned long. I'm not gonna play games. I'm done."

"But you should tell him that. You should talk to him, Whitney."

"It's too late." Whitney shrugged.

"It's not," Leslie argued. "He said he's called you a few times. Gets your voicemail. And you don't return his calls. And he said he saw you one night at the grocery store."

"Yeah. I waved at him."

"He said you looked like you didn't want to talk to him."

"I can't believe this. You, of all people, defending him."

"Nope, I'm not." Leslie scooted down the couch and reached for Whitney's hand. "I'm not. Just trying to make sure you think this through before it's too late."

"And by wanting me to think it through, you're suggesting I go to another party? With you and Asher."

"Well, Asher will probably be out of town, so I could go and be your date. And I totally swear I won't mind what you do. Won't feel you up later, either."

"And if someone hits on you?"

"You think anyone anywhere could outdo Asher for me?"

"Nope."

Leslie shrugged. "I'll hang out with Bronson. Or go downstairs and watch a movie. Or better yet, I could go hang out in the bed Asher slept in when he was staying with them. I could—"

"No." Whitney shook her head. "You go hang out and do whatever you feel like doing in that bed. But I'm not going."

8

Rather than go to the party—Whitney wouldn't even want to go to a *boring* party that involved nothing more exotic than drinking Long Island Iced Teas—Whitney and Leslie made plans to hang out over that weekend. Leslie had adjusted to Asher's sporadic travel schedule; she went with him when she could and stayed busy when she couldn't get away. But she missed him; in fact, if anyone was moping around these days, it was Leslie when Asher was gone.

Whitney didn't point that out to her friend, though. Because getting dragged back into that conversation was the last damned thing she wanted to do. She didn't want to admit to Leslie that Shawn had called her again. Twice. The first time she'd let it go to voicemail. The second, she hadn't been paying attention, and she'd answered the call without realizing it was Shawn.

They hadn't talked long. He asked how she was doing; she lied and said great, that she was staying busy. She told him about yoga and the book club. He didn't ask if she was seeing anyone; she didn't admit that she wasn't. She didn't ask him if he was dating; she couldn't bear the thought of him finding someone else. During the long hours in the night, when she was wide awake, her mind tended to venture down the crazy path that if Shawn met someone and fell in love, she might have to leave town. She couldn't watch him marry someone else. The thought of him being a father to someone else's children broke her heart all over again.

She also gave in on those long nights and looked at his social media accounts. The first time she'd gone to nose around after the break up, she'd held her breath, scared of what she would find. But there'd been little activity of any kind. Someone he worked with shared a news story with him about a new computer sales place in town. And his cousin posted a picture of an old car their grandpa owned when they were kids.

Nothing from Kori in Texas about that *awesome!! night.*

No new pictures of Shawn with other women. He hadn't even changed his status to single, but she hadn't, either.

They'd ended that one phone call with an awkward good-bye, Whitney dying to get away from him and Shawn sounding like he had more to say. She'd hung up and spent the rest of the night wondering what it might have been. What more could he have needed to say?

Her phone buzzed just before six. Leslie was heading over at any minute with pizza. Whitney had stocked up on beer. They'd planned a movie marathon, and to switch it up—Whitney had no interest in watching anything remotely romantic—they were going to watch slasher films. Whitney, dressed for comfort in gray leggings and a long white tunic, grabbed her phone from the counter and decided to get a head start on the beer. She'd stuck two in the freezer a while ago; she pulled one out now and twisted the top off as she glanced at her phone.

Gotta bail, Whit. I'm sorry.

"What?" Whitney took a long drink of the beer and then set the bottle down to answer Leslie's text.

What? Why? What's going on?

I've been throwing up all day.

WHAT?? No way.

Started after lunch. I thought it was just something I ate, but I can't keep anything down.

Are you lying? Did Asher stay here? Is that it? You're texting me from your bed?

No! I swear. I wish I was lying, and he was here.

Are you pregnant?

No way!! Ohmygod!! Stop!

Whitney sighed, frustrated that her weekend plans just went up in flames. She swallowed that down quickly and texted Leslie again.

I'll come to you. I'll bring you some soup.

Her phone buzzed in her hand, but someone tapped on the front door at the same time. She crossed the room slowly. Was Leslie jacking with her? Was she at the door with Asher? Maybe they were planning to kidnap her and make her go to the party? She'd thrown the invitation away.

"Are you kidding me? I'm not going. I told you I don't wanna—" She stopped talking when she found Shawn standing on the small porch. Hands buried in the hip pockets of his shorts, he hunched his shoulders and offered her a small, sheepish grin.

"You don't wanna what?" His low, gruff voice did things to her body, things she used to like. But now things he wasn't welcome to do. "Not going where?"

Whitney, stunned by the sudden turn of events, could only blink at him.

"Whit?" He tipped his head and raised his eyebrows in question.

"What're—? What're you doing here, Shawn?" Was he

finally here to get his stuff? But on a Friday night? Whitney had assumed he had better things to do.

"Are you busy? Do you have a date?"

"What?"

"Are you going to that party?"

"Party?" She shook her head. "What? What do you want?"

"Can we talk?"

Whitney's shoulders slumped, and she felt her heart slide, too. The weight of the last several weeks was heavy and burdensome. And of course, Leslie was right; she was still as in love with Shawn Green as she ever had been. But that didn't mean she was willing to go back to the way things were.

"I don't think so," she whispered. July evenings brought no relief from the heat and humidity, not in the Midwest, but Whitney—in her long sleeves and leggings—shivered under his intense stare.

"Is someone picking you up?" He twisted around to look over his shoulder. Whitney took the opportunity to feast her eyes on him, down over his hard, wide shoulders, his tight ass, and the lean but strong thighs that felt so good thrown over her legs, pinning her either in his bed or hers. She missed that, not just the sex, but lounging with him in bed or on the couch. Sharing their days or planning little things in their future.

That thought socked her in the gut. Shawn was always all in if they were planning a mini vacation or a weekend getaway. He enjoyed traveling, and he enjoyed site-seeing, and he liked sex. Even if he had looked for it with other women, Whitney knew he'd enjoyed sex with her. But he never wanted to plan too far into the future. They never talked about what sort of wedding they might have. No talk about a house or a family.

"Leslie said there was a party tonight." He turned back to her, his eyes a bit cool now. He looked at her the way he'd watched her at the bar the night of the party when Evan had kissed her and walked away. "Are you going?"

Whitney wondered what else he and Leslie had talked about.

"No."

"But you have a date? Someone's coming over?"

"Leslie was coming over," she admitted. She gave herself a mental shake. Yes, she still loved him, and yes, she was still attracted to him and right about now, she wanted to feel his lips on hers. She wanted to taste him. Even more than that, she wanted him to hold her.

But nothing had changed. And kissing him, making love to him now would only rob her of any progress she'd made since she'd asked him to let her go. Granted, it wasn't much, but she wasn't willing to take a step backwards.

"Can I come in? Please?"

Whitney met his eyes, now hot with need and emotion. Not anger. He wasn't looking for a repeat performance of the powder room sex the night of the party.

"I don't see the point in doing this," she said quietly. "I asked you to let me go."

"And I'm asking you to listen. Let me talk." He shrugged. "And then I'll go."

"I don't wanna hear it, Shawn. I don't want you to stand here and tell me you love me but. Okay? I want you to be happy, and I finally realized that what I want is never going to make you happy."

"Whitney? Can I come in?"

She sighed and stepped back to let him in.

"Why now?" She swung the door closed and folded her arms over her chest. She stayed by the door, to keep plenty of space between them. Shawn paced the living room, apparently lost in thought. She watched him smooth his hand over the back of the sofa before turning to look at her.

"I needed some time to think," he answered as he finally turned to her.

"Great." She nodded. "And did you have something to add? To the argument I've been having for three years now? You don't want to commit. You don't want me. You can't commit to me. I'm good enough until something better comes along? Which is it, Shawn? Just say it. Get it over with."

"I didn't touch anyone at that party."

She waited for him to continue, but he only stared at her.

"Okay." She shrugged when she realized he had nothing to add. "Is that it?"

"No!" He tossed his hands up helplessly. "No. God, I have so much I need to say, and I feel like I'm on a timer, and you're gonna kick me out if I can't say it all fast enough."

Whitney licked her lips and took a deep breath.

"Did you? Have sex with that guy? At the party?"

"Do you really think I would do that?"

"No. But."

Forgetting that she didn't want to get tangled up in this argument again, Whitney dropped her hands to her sides and crossed the room. She plopped on the end of the couch opposite of where he stood.

"No. I didn't. I talked to him. He held my hand and led me to a firepit in the backyard. And we talked. About how the parties work. How he and his wife deal with the things they do once they're home. He kissed me, Shawn." She shrugged. "But he's not you."

"It's okay," Shawn mumbled.

"What?"

"If you were with him, it's okay." He stepped around the end of the couch and perched on the edge of the cushion furthest away from her.

"It's not okay." She shook her head. "Dammit." She dabbed at her eyes when she realized she was crying. "It's not okay, and it's not okay that you would even say that."

"I mean, I wanted to punch the fucker in the face, Whit." Shawn shrugged. "The way he kissed you. In front of me. I wanted to kill him. But you looked...I don't know. You looked content. I could tell you liked the guy, and the last thing I wanted to do was cause a scene in front of people you work with."

"I liked the guy? What does that mean? He's a nice guy. He was one of the guys I kissed the night I played *Spin the Bottle* at the wedding shower. He approached me, and like I said, we talked."

"Sucker thought he was gonna get some." Shawn aimed a tiny grin at her. "You looked so hot that night. Your nipples in that dress made me so hard, I could've drilled through a fuckin' concrete wall with my dick."

"You kind of did," she reminded him. "Pounded me against that wall."

"Did I hurt you? Is that why you cried?"

"No." She shook her head. "You didn't hurt me. You've never hurt me like that."

"I drank a couple of beers. Talked to some girl for a while. She made plenty of offers, but I wasn't interested. Talked to the bartender for a while."

"Look, I get that you didn't enjoy the party. But that's not what this is about. It's not why I ended things."

"I didn't say I didn't enjoy it." He flopped back to rest on the couch. "I'm a guy. Of course, I enjoyed the scenery. I felt like I was an extra in a porn movie, Whit. And I would love to go to a party like that, knowing the woman I'm going to be with is my girlfriend. Not some random woman whose puzzle piece might interlock with mine."

Whitney blew out a deep sigh and ducked her chin to her chest.

"And I don't want to be your girlfriend anymore, Shawn."

"I just…" He groaned. "Jesus, Whitney, I love you. I don't want to *do life* without you. I hate waving at you at the grocery store. I hate that you're dodging my calls, and I know you are, so don't deny it. When did it change?"

"Nothing has changed. I'm always gonna love you. But I'm twenty-seven years old, Shawn. I'm done with dating. With sleepover sex. I need more. And what I need threatens you." She lifted her face to look at him and brushed the hair back from her eyes. "That leaves us nowhere to go."

"Part of me was hoping you were with that guy. At that party. That he took you somewhere private and did something incredible to you."

Shawn's quietly spoken words rendered her speechless. Paralyzed with sadness, she let her tears slide over her face as she watched him blink up at the ceiling. Finally, he rolled his head on the couch to look at her.

"I'm not being mean. I'm not trying to hurt you."

"Right." She nodded. As much as she hated the idea of going to another party at Frank and Donna's house, she decided she would rather be there right now than here, arguing—talking? Were they just talking?—with Shawn. She sniffled and licked her lips, hating the taste of salt. "I think you need to go."

"Not yet."

"Yeah, Shawn, now." She sounded tough, but inside, her belly and her heart were all tied up in knots. Her ribs squeezed painfully hard, and she fought to breathe. "I don't even know what I'm supposed to think right now. I just need you to go."

"I know I'm a dick to you sometimes, and I just thought… as much as I hated him, I thought you deserved someone to worship you. Just once. To give you everything."

"And all I ever wanted was for *you* to love me like that," she reminded him. "When I was talking to Evan, I wondered if that redhead was sucking your dick, and it killed me, Shawn. To think you would want someone else to do that."

When he didn't speak, Whitney climbed from her spot on the couch and paced across the room.

"That's the difference between me and you, I guess," she mumbled. "One difference, anyway. That's why I didn't want to go to the party in the first place."

"You could have warned me."

"I did," she reminded him. "You didn't listen."

"You said you played games at the shower."

Whitney shrugged. "I did, and I told you some of those games got pretty out of hand. And I had no idea what to expect the night we went together. But I didn't watch you walk away and hope that someone got down on her knees to worship you. Because I wanted you all to myself."

"The night in Texas."

Standing across the room at the window with her back to him, Whitney froze with one hand on the blinds. She shook her head, though, because she didn't want to know about the night in Texas. Not now. She didn't want to lay awake, alone, night after night and think about Shawn and some girl in Texas living it up and doing *awesome!!* things.

"Whit, I know you saw the picture on my wall." His voice was closer now. He'd moved; he was standing behind her. Trapped, Whitney swallowed down a rush of anger. "We broke up. Before that."

"Yeah, I know." She nodded. "And because you keep reminding me of that and because you thought that night with Kori was awesome, I'm just going to assume you fucked her. And I don't want to know."

"I didn't fuck her." His whisper was gruff, but Whitney heard a note of pain. She bit her lip, wishing he would go. Wishing he would take her in his arms. Wishing he wanted the same things in life that she did.

"Just go."

"Whitney." He rested his hands on her shoulders. "I didn't fuck her. She gave me a blowjob out by the car before we left. I know I shouldn't have done it. Shouldn't have let her do it. I'd had a few beers. I was angry with you. With me."

Whitney swiped at her eyes as she turned to look at him.

"Whatever, Shawn. We broke up before you left. And we're not together now, and so, I don't wanna know."

"That's why part of me wanted that guy to do you, to make you feel good—"

"To ease your guilty conscience." She nodded.

"I love you. I'm sorry. I know this is messed up. I know that. I know you want more out of a relationship than I've been willing to give you."

"Yeah. Well." She swallowed hard and shrugged. "I mean, we want different things. It was fun, Shawn. And I'm always gonna love you. But I can't do this anymore. I can't just be your girlfriend. I can't wait around for you to grow up and change your mind about what you want. Because I don't think you're going to. And I don't trust you, so there's nothing left."

"I've never cheated on you." He gripped her upper arms and rested his forehead on hers. "I have never been with someone else."

"Except Kori. Who put her mouth on your dick." She shrugged. "Which is pretty intimate."

"Whitney."

"Then again, that doesn't count, because we broke up before you left. I mean, we were separated for three whole days. So, you're totally in the clear for fucking around with some kid in Texas."

"I'm sorry. I made a mistake, and I hurt you."

"Okay." She shrugged and cleared her throat. "Is that it? Will you go now?"

"I don't want to go." He cupped her chin in his hand and pressed a kiss to her forehead.

"I need you to leave."

"Whitney, please? Forgive me?"

Eyes locked with his, Whitney took a slow, deep breath and then shook her head.

"If you love me," she could barely speak around the knife of emotion in her throat, "you'll let me go."

"I do love you, and I want a second chance."

"For what?" She lifted her arms to plant her hands on Shawn's chest. "For what? Why do we have to keep playing this same scene out?"

"Let's start over."

"No!" She shoved him backwards and watched him stumble before catching his footing.

"You can really just walk away? The past three weeks have been horrible without you."

His words were somewhat of a comfort, but when he moved toward her again, she stepped away from him.

"We've done all of this before."

"Not the—"

"Not the party. Not Texas." She waved his argument away. "But we've fought over the future and what we want. And every time we do, you kiss me, and you promise me you love me, and I just fall in line and keep my mouth shut."

His eyes were wet with unshed tears, but Whitney bit her

lip and steeled herself to those same empty promises. If she caved now, if she gave into him, she would only be reinforcing his belief that he could play her and string her along. Even if he loved her, it wasn't enough.

"I want more, Shawn. I deserve more than this."

9

He didn't back down. Whitney expected him to either step back or walk out—and she wouldn't stop him. Not even to tell him to get his things so he would have no reason to come back again—or cajole her into taking him back, into going back into the same go-nowhere relationship they'd been in for so long. Instead, Shawn nodded. His face was twisted in a painful-looking grimace, and his eyes were still wet; even his lashes were wet with tears.

"You do," he whispered. "You deserve so much more than what I've given you."

Stunned by his surrender, she could only stare at him suspiciously. Maybe he was going to play the I-love-you-but card. *I love you, but I can't give you what you need. I love you, but I don't want marriage. I never wanted to be a father.*

"Then let me go." She sniffled and pushed her hair back from her face. She didn't have much makeup on, but her face —her eyes—had to be wrecked. She wanted to crawl into bed alone and lick her wounds. And start over on the whole forgetting process. "Let me go. Because as long as I love you, as long as this hurts so much, I can't move on."

"I can't give you up."

"Shawn."

"I never said I was against marriage."

Disgusted with him for thinking he could still play her, and even more disgusted with herself for wanting him to feed her the right line to hook her again, Whitney rolled her eyes. With the wall at her back, she had nowhere to retreat, so she pushed past him and crossed back to the sofa on the other side of the room.

He hadn't. He had never said he didn't *believe* in marriage. His parents had recently celebrated their thirty-seventh anniversary. His brothers were happily married. From what Whitney could tell, he liked their wives. And he was great with his nephew.

But he was thirty years old, and he'd been dating Whitney since he was twenty-four, and he was good with keeping his toothbrush at her place.

"Don't do this." She shook her head and dashed at her nose and her eyes with the back of her hand. "Please. Don't do this to us."

"I watched my brothers get married, and I always just kind of figured I would do it one day. I never just decided it wasn't for me. I guess I just—"

"Please don't stand here and defend your choice to not marry me to me. You've made it clear you don't want that kind of commitment to me. This is only going to make me feel worse, Shawn."

"I never said I don't want to be committed to you!" This time, when he threw his hands up, Whitney could read the anger in the hard set of his jaw. "I love you. I loved you from the night we went to that music festival downtown, and we drank that horrible apple cider from the plastic cup we had to share because they were running low. You were wearing skinny jeans and a blue sweater, and your laugh was better than any music we heard. And then the band—they were terrible, by the way, we both thought so—started singing that Damien Rice song. You knew every word."

Whitney covered her mouth, but a small sob slipped out. She remembered the night. They'd listened to every last song that band played, and they *had* been terrible. But the *night* had been perfect with the hint of fall in the air, and Shawn's arm around her, his face pressed close to hers most of the night.

"You loved me then?"

"Yes." He nodded. "I loved you then. And I knew that you were it. You're the one. And if my not putting a ring on your finger is what's gonna tear us apart, I'm sorry. I've been too busy loving our life together to think about rings—"

"It's not the ring, Shawn," she whispered. "It's not the ring. It's not the big wedding and the dress and cake."

He stared at her from across the room, brows arched in question.

"I don't need that. I don't need a big dress. I don't need a diamond. I need you."

"You've had me. You have had me from day one. I hate the fights. I hate it, Whitney. I hate what I did to you when I was in Texas, and I'm so damned sorry. You throwing me out of here after the party hurt more than anything I've ever felt. I want you in my life."

"And I can't do it." She dropped to sit on the sofa. Elbows on her knees, she buried her face in her hands. "I can't meet you for dinner on Tuesday nights and sleep over at your place on Thursday and maybe know that I'll see you Saturday."

"I'm not gonna let you go."

"One house. Your name. Your babies. Our dreams." She lifted her face to look at him. "That's what I want."

Shawn sighed and cleared his throat. Whitney watched

him pace the floor in front of her. He stacked his hands behind his head as he walked; the movement pulled his shirt up to expose tan skin over his flat abs. She jerked her gaze from the waistband of his shorts. She wanted that, too, but not if it didn't come with the heart and the soul of the man it was attached to.

"You don't want kids?" She licked her lips. "Is that it?"

"Sure I do," he mumbled as he padded back across the floor. "It's all just stuff I thought I—we had more time for. And if I tell you that now, if I tell you I want this, that I want my forever to be with you, you're just gonna think I'm placating you. That I'm talking out of both sides of my mouth and that I'll never get around to making any changes."

She nodded when he glanced at her in askance.

"Yeah."

"And if I get down on one knee and ask you to marry me, you'll accuse me of rushing into this part of it, and you'll say no."

"If you ask me to marry you when you don't really want that, you'll only end up resenting me. You'll feel like I'm tying you down. I don't wanna be your ball and chain. Not anymore."

He stopped walking and simply stared at her.

"So, what do I do? What can I do to keep you? Because after watching you walk away from me with another guy to go and do private, sexy things, I refuse to lose you."

"Is that what it took? For you to decide to keep me?"

When she blinked, hot tears streaked her cheeks.

"Don't do that," he argued. He let his hands fall to his sides and moved back toward her. Dropping to his knees in front of her, he cupped her upper arms in his hands. "You know I love you. You *know* that."

She nodded. "But never enough to keep me. To make it official. To give me your name."

"Please believe me." He kissed her cheek. "I don't know what I have to do. I don't know what you want to call it. Starting over. Picking up the pieces. Moving forward. But please let me be in your life."

Whitney smoothed her hand over his face, her thumb pressing into his lips. She hadn't planned to touch him, but the need to feel his skin was too powerful to ignore.

"I don't know if I have anything left to give, Shawn," she whispered.

"I was thinking about our places." He covered her hand on his face with his and then moved hers so he could press a kiss to the palm of her hand. "I don't know how you feel about it, but yours is definitely better. You have a spare bedroom, and I don't. You have a backyard. And I know you hate how small my bathroom is."

She pulled her hand away from him and balled her fingers into a fist.

"We could live here. For a while. And when we feel like we're ready, we could find something bigger. Newer."

When she didn't answer him—she couldn't speak around her heart in her throat—he tipped his head and rushed to continue.

"Or older. I know you like old farmhouses. We could find a place like that and do... some updating. If you want. Then we'd have a bigger yard. I just—I'd rather be making a mortgage payment than paying rent. At our age."

She'd thrown that argument at him a time or ten through the past several years, too. Now, she blinked at him, uncertain about his motives.

"We could sell everything and run away and join the circus, for all I care, Whitney Oliver." His intense gaze made her squirm. "As long as we do it together."

"I'd never ask you to give up the things you do." Her hand was on his face again, her fingers drawing on his skin and reading memories they'd made together. "I just want to share our lives. I hate the nights when you're not here. When we don't sleep together. I hate waking up without you. I'm sorry that it threatens you. That words like *husband* and *wife*—"

"We could elope," he suggested. "Right now."

"Can't." She shook her head. "No marriage license. And also, Leslie would kill me."

"She's not sick." Shawn traced his finger over her nose. "I asked her to lie and say she was, so I could talk to you."

"What if this doesn't work, Shawn? I can't do this again. I can't break again, because I lose a little bit of myself every time I do. I won't be whole again."

"It's gonna work," he promised.

Still hesitant to give in—he'd changed his approach, but she still wasn't convinced he would commit—Whitney turned her head a bit when he moved to kiss her. His lips pressed to the corner of her mouth and lingered there. Her heart reveled in his warmth, and her body remembered all the incredible things he did to it. But her brain waved the red flag, warning her to be cautious. If he took her to bed and got up and went back to his place in the morning, she would be the same fool she'd been for years.

"I dream about you." He kissed a trail from her lips to her ear. Whitney sighed when he flicked her earlobe with the tip of his tongue. "I dream about you in that green dress. Taking you against the wall like that."

"Shawn." She rested her forehead on his shoulder.

"I wish I would have taken it off you."

"What?"

"The dress. That five minutes in the bathroom with you was the best five minutes of the night. No question, and Whit, I saw a lot of action at the pool."

"Imagine being Bronson," she mumbled.

"You can't even imagine." His lips skated over her face

again, lingering on her cheek and her forehead and then back at her mouth. "But all I've thought about is the time with you. I wish I would have taken my time. Taken that dress off of you. The thought of you in the heels and that thong? Your nipples hard and ready for my mouth? I should have put my tongue inside you. Tasted you again. I miss that, Whitney."

Tears burned in her eyes again. She tipped her head, rested against his chin, and closed her eyes.

"I miss holding you." His warm breath tickled her ear. "Waking up with you in my arms."

He pressed his lips to her neck again and slid the fingers of his right hand up into her hair.

"Me, too," she admitted.

"Do you miss making love? To me?" He drew back to look at her. When she refused to look at him, he hooked her chin with the fingers of his left hand and forced her to look up.

"I do." Her voice was thick with tears. "But I don't want you in my bed tonight. Because I don't believe anything will be different tomorrow."

"I will give you everything," he whispered. "Everything, Whitney. I just need you to trust me. Let me prove it. Let me be there tomorrow. And the day after."

Her throat still tight with tears, she licked her lips. Opened her mouth to answer him, but before she could swallow the emotion and find her voice, Shawn kissed her. His tongue was gentle but bold, dipping deep and slow in her mouth. She held back, not out of spite, but need. She let him kiss her, aware of the sensation of his hot, wet tongue smoothing over hers, around her teeth, and stroking the roof of her mouth.

"Kiss me." He pulled away from her long enough to make the demand. She parted her lips again, meeting his tongue with hungry strokes of her own. She was wet, aware that Shawn would smell her arousal, but she didn't fight him. Not now. Her inner thighs, her clit throbbed with the need for him to fill her completely, and nothing short of making love with him would satisfy her.

Unaware that she had lifted her hands again to rest them on his shoulders, she dug her fingernails into him and held on. His mouth still hot on hers, she felt his hands move and then slowly, he inched her tunic up over her stomach. She moaned softly when he stopped, right hand pinning her shirt to her chest, his left hand rubbing slow and steady over her belly.

"Shawn."

"No." He shook his head. "I'm not gonna rush through this, Whitney."

"I want—"

"Ssh." He drew away, dragged his gaze down over her body, and then let go of her shirt to smooth his hands over her thighs. Whitney held her breath for a moment and then let it go in a big gush of need when he pushed her thighs apart and rubbed his thumb between her legs.

"Touch me." She arched her brows hopefully. Shawn leaned into her to brush his lips over hers, but he moved quickly down her body. Hands pushing her legs open wide, he buried his face at her center.

"Shawn."

"Can you feel this?" His low, gruff voice shot a jolt of desire through her. She felt the pressure on her clit, but through the knit leggings and her panties, it wasn't enough.

"Yes." She tucked her chin to her chest and watched him lick her there, still with the clothing between them. "Gimme more?"

He lifted his head and met her gaze, his eyes hot with need.

"I need to see these." He cupped her breasts in his hands. Eyes still locked with hers, he pressed her nipples with his thumbs. Again, she moaned with pleasure and need. "Can I look at you? I wanna see your nipples, Whit. I want to suck on you and bite you and then lick them and blow on you and soothe them. Can I do that?"

"Please." Her sharp, desperate whisper spurred him into action. Hands still moving too slowly for her, she watched for a moment as he pushed her shirt up and then finally, she grabbed it and whipped it over her head. She let it fall to the floor behind her and then sat, arms over her head, as Shawn pressed his face between her breasts.

Her nipples ached for his touch, but he only teased her, fingers fluttering and feathering over the silk cups of her bra. She cried out in protest when he opened his mouth over the silk, rather than moving it aside to taste her skin.

"I think you should take this off," he suggested.

"I agree." She nodded and moved quickly. Shawn sucked the silk and her nipple into his mouth as she arched her back to unhook the offending material and remove it. Without lifting his head, he slipped the straps over her arms and plucked the silk away from her.

Rather than taste her, rather than suck her nipple into his mouth, rather than nipping at her sensitive skin, he drew back and looked up at her.

"Please. Shawn?"

"I want you to put your shirt on." His eyes were hot and intense as he dragged them over her neck and then her breasts. She didn't think it was possible, but she felt them tighten again under his heated gaze. "I wanna see that again."

"No." She sobbed and shook her head.

"I wanna see these gorgeous tits and nipples hard under that shirt. Maybe wet. You had every goddamned guy at that party drooling over your tits."

"I need you to touch me," she argued. Slowly, his gaze climbed from her breasts back over her lips and up to meet her eyes. When he didn't move, she lifted her hands and pinched the tight ruby red beads. "Suck them, Shawn."

"I want them on my cock."

"Take your pants off," she said simply.

"Not yet."

He watched her fingers for a moment, though he knew how she liked to be touched. Still, she loved that he wanted to watch her. He always had. Now, he dipped his head and circled her nipple with the tip of his tongue. Before she could slide her hands over her stomach, he licked her fingers and then turned his attention to her other breast.

With her hands and his mouth on her breasts, his hands were free to roam. Whitney moaned softly when he hooked his fingers in her leggings and started edging them down over her hips. Surrendering to the tug of his lips on her nipple, she gasped in surprise when he sank his teeth into her sensitive skin. She lifted her bottom from the couch so he could wiggle the leggings down further.

His hungry, skilled mouth on her breasts, Whitney clutched his shoulders and then combed her fingers up through the back of his hair to hold his head there. She expected him to take her leggings all the way down, but he stopped at mid-thigh.

"Shawn." She struggled to open her legs wider when he rubbed his knuckles over her clit.

"Let me do this my way." He tipped his head and quirked one brow at her. "I wanna make you beg, Whitney. I wanna make you scream for me."

His eyes steady on hers, she caught her breath when he rubbed that knuckle over her clit again and then pressed the pad of his thumb into her wet folds.

"You're wet." She watched him lift his hand to his mouth and lick his knuckle and then his thumb, the slow drag of his tongue suggestive. Whitney wiggled on the couch, a soft whimper escaping her lips. "I missed this. I missed your pussy, Whitney. You know how I love to kiss you there."

Her mind threw up that picture, the one of him and his Texas girl.

"What's wrong?" he asked immediately, as if he sensed that she was upset.

"Did you kiss her there? The Texas girl?"

"No." He shook his head. "I haven't had my lips on another woman's body since I met you. I promise you that."

She nodded, but her eyes filled again.

"Whitney?"

"Okay."

"Can I touch you?"

"Yes."

The last time he'd touched her, he'd driven his cock hard and deep inside her and ridden her mercilessly until they'd both come, panting and gasping for air. Tonight, his touch was soft and gentle. Leggings still around her thighs, her legs parted just enough to see the delta of dark curls over her sex, Shawn rubbed his thumb over her clit again, back and forth and back and forth again. Whitney sank into the sofa, the pressure of his thumb on her clit as arousing as it was frustrating.

He played there, hungry eyes watching his thumbs spread her open and stroke and pinch and gently probe her sensitive skin.

"Feel good?" He flicked his eyes up to meet hers.

"Yes."

Eyes still locked with hers, he eased his finger inside her. When she squirmed on the couch and managed to open her legs further, he added a second and then a third finger. She dropped her head back to rest on the couch. She had wanted his cock buried as deep as it would go. Barring that, she wanted his mouth on her.

But this—the stretching, rubbing motion of his fingers inside her—felt too damned good to rush him.

"I wish you could see yourself." He dragged his left hand over her nude upper body, smoothing her belly and her breasts and her neck. "You're beautiful."

"I'm not gonna come like this, Shawn," she whispered.

"Does it feel good?"

"So fucking good." She closed her eyes. "But if you don't touch my clit, I'm not gonna come."

"Whit, I know your body, babe," he reminded her. "I'll make you come."

"Is this boring for you?" She lifted her head to look at him. "Just putting your fingers inside me?"

"Are you kidding me? Can you see my dick right now? Your pussy's so hot and wet and tight on my fingers. The way it feels on my cock. I can't wait to sink inside you. You know what that's gonna feel like?"

"What?"

"Home."

She pressed her lips together and stared at him. The familiar ache built slowly, the repeated motion of Shawn's fingers inside her drawing the tension tighter.

"Touch them." He nodded.

"What about tomorrow?" she whispered, but she couldn't fight the flames of desire that burned inside her. She rubbed her hands up over her stomach and her breasts and then, unable to wait, she pinched her nipples and rolled them between her thumbs and fingers.

"I thought Asher might help me move some stuff over here."

It crossed her mind to argue. To tell him that Asher was out of town. But as if he sensed how close she was to climaxing, he pressed his thumb hard over her clit and moved it in big, slow circles, his fingers still pumping inside her.

She wasn't a screamer. She called out his name, she'd always called out for him when he drove her to orgasm. This time, his name started on her lips as a chant that she repeated over and over as he pushed her to fly apart. When the ball of tension inside exploded, and she threw her head back and tensed her shoulders and her stomach and her ass cheeks, Shawn kept his fingers inside her and stroked her through the orgasm.

She gasped when she felt his tongue on her left breast. He traced the heavy curve and then zeroed in on her nipple, closing his lips to tug hard on her wet, tight skin.

"Come again, Whit." He nipped her, tugged hard on her nipple with his teeth, and pinched her other nipple hard with the fingers of his free hand. A ball of flame exploded again in her core, and her scream of pleasure and pain ripped through the otherwise quiet room.

10

W hitney's body quivered with aftershocks as Shawn slipped his fingers from inside her, still massaging her swollen, sensitive areas as he moved. Breathless and physically sated, she watched through hooded eyes as he stood and unzipped his shorts. Her thighs were still bound in the leggings, and she wanted to protest, to shove them down and out of the way. But her limbs were thick and heavy, so she simply watched as Shawn unveiled his body. Shorts loose around his waist, he whipped his shirt over his head and dropped it at his feet. Whitney's eyes traveled over his wide shoulders and his smooth, muscular chest. She loved kissing him there, sucking on his flat brown nipples, but again, she didn't move.

Her eyes followed his hands to his shorts, hungry to see the rest of him. He pushed his shorts and his briefs down, exposing his hips. His long, thick cock jutted proudly, and Whitney fought to shove the Texas thing from her mind. This man belonged to her. She knew how to take care of him, to pleasure him, and the thought of that skinny little girl in Texas—at least she was legal to drink, because she'd had a beer in her hand in the photo—thinking she could offer him anything better made her angry.

Shawn stepped out of the shorts and briefs and kicked them aside. Before Whitney could speak, he removed her leggings and tossed them aside, too. Gaze locked with his, she reached up and cupped his balls in her hand.

He moaned with pleasure when she sat up and licked him from his sac to the tip of his cock.

"This is mine," she reminded him. "All for me."

"It is." He smoothed his fingers through her hair. "But I'm not done with you yet."

"Did she do it like I do? Did she swallow?"

"Lean back." He eased her back against the couch. Eyes hot with tears again, Whitney watched him part her legs again, only this time she was unencumbered by her clothing. Shawn dug his fingers into her thighs and kissed her, his lips soft over hers. Whitney kissed him back, scared suddenly that he was logging the details of their lovemaking to compare them to someone, something else.

"Let me do you," she whispered when he drew back. "Let me—"

"Sshh." He shook his head. "Hang on, babe."

Hands on her hips he tugged her forward on the couch, so that she balanced on the edge of the cushion. Whitney watched him as he used his thumbs to spread her open. He kneaded her folds, teased her with a quick flick of his fingertip over her clit, and then blew on her. She moaned softly as his warm breath hit her wet heat. Chills climbed her spine, and her nipples tingled and beaded again.

He lifted his eyes to look at her; the heat in his stare caught fire over her skin. Whitney, naked and completely exposed to him, dragged her teeth over her lower lip as she anticipated his next move. Rather than kiss her there, he straightened on his knees and pressed his open mouth to the under curve of her left breast. She wound her arms around his neck as he sucked her skin into his mouth, sure to leave a mark.

"I've been thinking about this since you asked me to leave."

"Sex?"

"Making love." He licked a path from her breast to her belly button. "With you."

She played with his hair and then stroked her fingernails down over his bare shoulders.

"Did you think of me? At all?"

"Yes." Of course, she did.

"What did you miss most?"

"Lying in your arms," she said when he lifted his head and met her eyes. "After we make love."

"Did you miss the orgasms? At all?" He gave her a cheeky grin.

"Yes."

"Did you play with your vibrator?"

"Mmm. Shawn."

"So, maybe you didn't miss me that much?"

"I did."

"Your vibrator's pretty fancy," he argued. "But there are some things it can't do."

"I know."

"Touch yourself, Whit."

She did as he asked, as she'd been aching to do. One hand covered her breast and the other, she slid between her legs to rub her fingers over her clit. Shawn watched her for a moment. He sat back on his feet and stroked his hand over his cock. Whitney licked her lips when he rubbed his thumb in a circle over his head. Pre-cum glistened on his engorged skin. He raised his hand and pressed it to her lips. She sucked his thumb into her mouth, her fingers still working her own body.

"I'm gonna do all those things your vibrator doesn't." He arched his brow as he tweaked her nipple. "Starting with that right there. Those pretty girls don't get much out of your vibrator."

She knew he was working his way down, and she nearly wept with anticipation and need.

"Shawn." She moaned when he kissed her breast, careful to lick her everywhere but over her nipple.

"I'm gonna lick you, Whitney. I'm gonna flick your clit with the tip of my tongue."

He nudged her nipple instead.

"And then I'm gonna rub it with my tongue, like this."

"Please?" She lifted her lips from the couch, her inner thighs pressed to the hot skin of his chest. "Please? I can't wait, Shawn."

"And I'm going to drag my teeth over your clit." He moved to her other breast and nipped at her. "And your lips. I'm gonna thrust my tongue inside you, and then I'm gonna suck your clit into my mouth."

Whitney rubbed her mound against his chest and wrapped her fingers around the back of his head. He stopped her when she tried to circle her legs around his back.

"Nope." He put his hands on her thighs again and spread her open. "I want you just like this. Wide open. You're dripping wet, Whitney."

She sighed and swallowed hard when he dipped his finger just inside her and then withdrew it. He leaned in again and pressed that same finger to her lips, waiting for her to shove him away. Instead, she licked him, knowing it turned him on that she would taste herself on his skin.

He teased her with his thumb and trailed his wet finger back over her breast and her belly. Without further comment, he slipped both hands under her thighs to tilt her sex up to his face and flicked his tongue over her clit.

Whitney moved her hips, desperate to get closer to him, but he held her firmly to press her legs wide open. She dropped her head back to rest on the sofa as he licked her clit and her folds and the creases where her thighs met her center. His tongue was relentless over her most sensitive skin, first with gentle nudges and then with increasing pressure.

Her nipples ached as the knot of tension built between her legs. Shawn's fingers massaged her thighs as his tongue massaged her clit. She thrashed on the sofa when he tilted her hips further and plunged his tongue inside her, lapping at her excitement. He pressed his thumbs into her ass cheeks and rubbed gently, and then he moved to suck her clit into his mouth and thrust his fingers inside her.

She came hard, her head thrown back in pleasure and her thighs closing in on his face. Still he worked her skin with his teeth and his tongue, and Whitney yanked a handful of his hair even as she pushed him closer.

When he drew back, she watched him climb to his feet. His cock strained toward her, hard and ready to take her. Rather than wait, rather than kill the moment, she turned on the couch and lifted her ass in offering. Without hesitating, Shawn grabbed her by the hips and thrust into her from behind.

"Not gonna take much," he told her.

"I want your cock on me." She moved her hips with his, squeezing hard to milk him. "On my tits. In my mouth."

"Fuck, Whitney." He slowed his movements and held her still for a moment. "I don't wanna come yet. You feel too fucking good, and it's been too fucking long."

"Do it, Shawn." She wiggled her hips against his. "Do it. We can do it again."

"Another five seconds of my mouth between your legs, and I would've come. All over your couch."

"I like your couch better," she promised him. "Fuck me."

He gripped her hips hard and pulled out to drive his cock inside her again. She held on to the back of the couch as he quickened the pace and finally exploded inside her.

They collapsed to the couch together; Shawn pressed into her backside, her front draped over the back of the couch.

"Come to bed with me," she whispered. "Stay here tonight."

"Let's go." He pressed a chaste kiss to the back of her neck. Whitney turned her head, searching to meet his gaze, but he moved. Backed off the couch and then helped her to stand. She glanced at the front door, but he linked his fingers with hers and shook his head. "Go on to bed. I'll lock up."

She didn't comment on the early hour. If Shawn was going to climb into her bed with her now and spend the rest of the night pleasuring her, she wasn't going to argue. They'd spent nights like this before, hours and hours of lovemaking only to stop and say goodbye because one of them had to go home for one reason or other. Whitney could only pray that this time would be different.

She padded bare foot to the hall and then looked over her shoulder to watch him. All hard muscles under smooth, tan skin—except for the private spots only she was supposed to see—he was a beautiful man. She thought again of the video they'd made, how surprised she'd been at how sensual the two of them were together. Shawn's body was perfection, and while she wasn't a woman to belittle herself, she'd been more than fascinated with her face and the look of extreme satisfaction that Shawn had put there.

Satisfied that the house was locked up, Shawn turned to follow her to the bedroom. Even after sex, after the orgasm, his cock was still impressive as he crossed the room. He left the lamp on, ignored the TV, eyes focused only on her.

"I love you." He slid his arm around her waist as they made their way to the bedroom.

"Asher's out of town," she told him as they crossed the threshold to her room.

"Is it gonna be a problem if I ask you to ditch the pink in here?" He flipped the lamp on and looked around. There wasn't a lot of pink. Accent pillows. A framed abstract painting of some sort on the wall.

"No." She stood on her tiptoes and looped her arms around his neck. "But I'm not good with the brown plaid comforter on your bed."

"Okay." He settled his hands on her hips and dropped a kiss on the tip of her nose. "Maybe just you. Naked. Tied to our bed? What do you think about that?"

"You'd never have to tie me to anything, Shawn." She rested her cheek on his chest. "I'd stay there just for you."

"There's one other thing."

"What?"

"If we get pregnant?"

"Are you sure you wanna do this? Because if you wake up tomorrow and change your mind, you're going to kill me. Please don't hurt me like that again."

Shawn cupped her chin in his hand and forced her to look at him.

"Well." He frowned. "Two things actually. Twins run in our family. My aunt and uncle are twins," he reminded her. She nodded and laughed softly. "And my mom will insist if we have a boy, we have to name him after my grandfather."

Whitney had never met Shawn's grandparents; they'd all been gone when they started dating. She tipped her head and frowned.

"Okay?"

"Not okay," he argued and shook his head dramatically. "His name was Leopold."

"Leo's not so bad, Shawn," she whispered.

"Whit?"

"Hmm?"

"Remember those things you said you wanted in the other room?"

"Your cock? In my mouth? Between my tits?"

He gave her a lecherous grin and wagged his eyebrows. "Give me a minute, and I'll be ready to collect on that. But no. I meant…the house…my name. Babies. Dreams."

Her throat tight, she could only nod.

"I want all of it. And it's only ever been you."

SNEAK PEEK AT SEALED WITH A KISS, STORY #3

Wild Canyon Estates Party.

Evan Bellinger had seen the notification pop on his phone calendar; he'd been watching it get closer every day. It used to be he almost dreaded these nights. He knew most guys would love the free pass to flirt with and fuck other women —younger, older, blondes, redheads, skinny, and curvy, too— but that free pass was for everyone. Not as much fun when your wife was at the same party, doing God knows what with any number of guys that weren't you.

Knowing that it took hooking up with someone else for his wife to get off had been a huge blow to Evan's ego. Janie had been a firecracker in bed back in the day. She was limber and adventurous, and she was always eager to please. But she hadn't gotten the same pleasure out of their sex life that he had, and while he'd known that, it wasn't something they really talked about as a couple. Rather than deal with it head on, they had skirted around the issue for too many years, and Janie had found her sexual pleasure with her fingers or her vibrator.

That was bad enough. But when she'd come home with

an invite to a party at her coworker's house and hinted to Evan that it sounded very adultish and a little risqué and even a bit forbidden, he knew it would be a problem. If that first conversation about the parties had plagued him with dread, actually *going* to that first party had been sheer hell. Janie, with her blond hair and big blue eyes, had taken fifty by storm. She was a knockout when they met; Evan thought she was even prettier with a touch of age and wisdom in her face. Petite and slightly curvy—Evan loved the curve of her hips and her full breasts—Janie had a personality bigger than the state of Texas. She was fun, and her boisterous laugh turned every head in the room.

No question the parties—the sexual freedom—suited her. He had promised her that first night that he was okay with whatever happened; he loved her far too much to begrudge her the pleasure he hadn't been able to deliver nearly often enough. But watching other men want his wife, and watching his wife play with other men had been a hell of a lot harder than he had ever imagined. There were pluses— not even including his very own free pass. Seeing other men come on to Janie had reminded Evan just how sexy his wife was, and with a whole new playground of opportunity, Janie had learned to relax with him when they were alone together at home. But he still thought it strange to say sex with other partners had saved his sex life, maybe his marriage—because who knew? It was possible, wasn't it, that once the boys were grown and gone, Janie might pack her bags and walk out in search of something better?

ABOUT THE AUTHOR

TE Sheridan is the author of thirty women's fiction and contemporary romance novels. She lives in the Midwest with her husband and two children.

ALSO BY TE SHERIDAN

Goodnight Kisses, Wild Canyon Estates Stories, #1

www.ingramcontent.com/pod-product-compliance
Lightning Source LLC
Chambersburg PA
CBHW030553130626
46552CB00006B/2534